Enjoy all of these American Girl Mysteries:

THE SILENT STRANGER   A *Kaya* Mystery

PERIL AT KING'S CREEK   A *Felicity* Mystery

TRAITOR IN WILLIAMSBURG   A *Felicity* Mystery

SECRETS IN THE HILLS   A *Josefina* Mystery

THE RUNAWAY FRIEND   A *Kirsten* Mystery

SHADOWS ON SOCIETY HILL   An *Addy* Mystery

THE CURSE OF RAVENSCOURT   A *Samantha* Mystery

THE STOLEN SAPPHIRE   A *Samantha* Mystery

DANGER AT THE ZOO   A *Kit* Mystery

MIDNIGHT IN LONESOME HOLLOW   A *Kit* Mystery

A THIEF IN THE THEATER   A *Kit* Mystery

A SPY ON THE HOME FRONT   A *Molly* Mystery

THE LIGHT IN THE CELLAR   A *Molly* Mystery

— A *Kit* MYSTERY —

A THIEF IN
THE THEATER

by Sarah Masters Buckey

★ American Girl®

Questions or comments? Call 1-800-845-0005, visit our Web site
at **americangirl.com**, or write to Customer Service, American Girl,
8400 Fairway Place, Middleton, WI 53562-0497.

Printed in China
08 09 10 11 12 13 LEO 10 9 8 7 6 5 4 3

PICTURE CREDITS
The following individuals and organizations have generously given permission to
reprint illustrations contained in "Looking Back": pp. 172–173—theaters, photo by
Dan Finfrock. Reprinted with permission from *Stepping Out in Cincinnati* by
Allen J. Singer. Available from the publisher online at www.arcadiapublishing.com
or by calling 888-313-2665; boy with popcorn, © Michael Ochs Archives/Corbis;
pp. 174–175—girls in front row, © Hulton-Deutsch Collection/Corbis; theater front,
Denver Public Library, Western History Collection; Tarzan, © Sunset Boulevard/
Corbis; pp. 176–177—boys with radio, © Underwood & Underwood/Corbis;
Orphan Annie cover, Little Orphan Annie® and © Tribune Media Services, Inc.; theater
marquee, © Peter Turnley/Corbis; FTP outdoor play, Corbis; pp. 178–179—1936
production of *Macbeth*, Library of Congress, Federal Theatre Project; *Macbeth* poster,
Corbis; cat in dressing room, © Hulton-Deutsch Collection/Corbis; modern *Macbeth*
performance, © Bob Krist/Corbis.

Illustrations by Jean-Paul Tibbles

Library of Congress Cataloging-in-Publication Data.

Buckey, Sarah Masters, 1955–
A thief in the theater / by Sarah Masters Buckey : [illustrations by Jean-Paul Tibbles].
p. cm "A Kit mystery"
Summary: In 1935, while preparing to write a newspaper story about a theater
production of Macbeth in her hometown of Cincinnati, twelve-year old Kit discovers
that a thief is stealing from the box office.
ISBN 978-1-59369-294-0 (pbk.) — ISBN 978-1-59369-295-7 (hardcover)
[1. Theater—Fiction. 2. Newspapers—Fiction. 3. Robbers and outlaws—Fiction.
4. Mystery and detective stories. 5. Cincinnati (Ohio)—History—20th century—
Fiction.] I. Tibbles, Jean-Paul, ill. II. Title.

PZ7.B87983Th 2008   [Fic]—dc22   2007042360

For Alice Boyle

TABLE OF CONTENTS

1

A JOB TO DO

Waves of heat shimmered from the pavement as Kit Kittredge stood guard for her friend Stirling Howard. It was so hot that Kit could feel the sizzling concrete through her thin-soled shoes.

"How many papers do you still have to sell?" she asked Stirling, who was standing on the street corner just a few feet away.

Stirling glanced at the big canvas bag hanging from his shoulder. "Only a few," he reported. "It shouldn't take long if—"

Just then, a Model T slowed at the intersection. "Get your newspaper!" Stirling called, his voice surprisingly deep for a short, skinny kid. "Read Cincinnati's latest news!"

The black Model T passed by. So did the

next five or six cars.

Kit shaded her eyes from the sun and looked up and down the nearby streets. The searing August afternoon was coming to a close, and Kit saw Mr. Petrowski pulling in the awning over his barbershop. Further down the street, Mr. Maggiano was putting away the fruits and vegetables on display in front of his grocery store.

"The stores are closing—we'd better go home soon," Kit told Stirling. "I've got to work on my job, too."

Kit and Stirling were both working for newspapers this summer, but in different ways—and for different papers. Stirling wanted to earn money, and he was selling newspapers for the *Cincinnati Daily Herald*. Kit dreamed of being a reporter, and she was writing articles for the children's page of the *Cincinnati Register*.

Kit planned to write her next article about the play *A Midsummer Night's Dream*. She and Stirling were going to see the play tonight at the nearby Burns Theater, and Kit could hardly wait. This was going to be her last newspaper assignment for the summer, and she wanted it to be her best yet.

"I'll try to hurry," Stirling promised her. He looked around nervously. "You don't see the boys I told you about, do you?"

"No," said Kit. "But I'm watching."

Stirling continued to wave copies of the *Cincinnati Daily Herald,* and he yelled "Newspapers!" louder than ever. Finally, a long tan Studebaker rolled to a stop at the corner. The driver handed Stirling a dime. As Stirling was fumbling to give the man a nickel in change, Kit saw three husky blond boys far down the street. Walking side by side and swinging their arms, the boys were hogging most of the sidewalk as they made their way up the street.

Kit eyed the boys watchfully. Several times over the past weeks, Stirling had been bullied by a group of boys. At first, the bullies had just snatched a newspaper from Stirling's bag.

Then the boys had begun to demand that Stirling give them money for the privilege of selling his newspapers on the street. The last time that Stirling had met up with the boys, he'd come home with an empty newspaper bag—and empty pockets.

"I worked for hours," he had told Kit, his voice trembling with anger. "And all I have left is two pennies!"

Stirling had described the bullies to Kit as "three big blond kids." Now she called to him as the Studebaker drove away. "Look behind you," she warned.

Stirling whirled around. As soon as he caught sight of the boys, his face went pale. "It's them! We've got to get out of here!"

Holding tight to his canvas bag, Stirling took off down the street. Kit was close behind him. She looked back over her shoulder and saw that the three blond boys had started running, too. The bullies were still a couple of blocks away, but they were catching up fast.

Earlier in the afternoon, Kit and Stirling

had worked out an escape route. Now they put their plan into action. Racing down the street, they rushed past some kids playing marbles and then dove into the cool shade of Maggiano's Grocery Store.

The screen door closed behind them with a loud *thwap*. Mrs. Maggiano, a tiny, gray-haired woman, was standing at the cash register carefully counting out coins. She was one of Stirling's regular customers, and she looked up at him with a smile. "You're in a hurry today!"

"Yes, ma'am," said Stirling breathlessly. He handed her a copy of the *Cincinnati Daily Herald*. Then he and Kit started down the narrow aisles, past the rows of sweet-smelling apples and pears and toward the rear of the store.

"Where you going?" Mrs. Maggiano called to them. "We're about to close."

Kit and Stirling stopped short. "We thought," gasped Stirling, still out of breath, "that we'd use the back door."

"It's quicker," Kit explained.

Mrs. Maggiano glanced out the store's big plate-glass window. "I see three of the Hobart boys coming this way. Those boys are always causing trouble." She turned to Stirling and fixed him with a sharp eye. "Do they have anything to do with your hurry?"

There was an uncomfortable silence. Kit and Stirling looked at each other, but neither said a word.

Mrs. Maggiano nodded toward the back of the store. "Go on," she said. "And if those boys come in here looking for you, I'll give 'em a piece of my mind."

Kit and Stirling tore out the back door and sprinted down the long alley behind the store. They didn't stop running until they came to the street at the other end of the alley. Then, walking as fast as they could without drawing attention to themselves, they hurried down the busy street, looking over their shoulders to make sure they weren't being followed.

After two blocks, they turned onto a quiet avenue. At the end of the next block, they turned again. Now Kit could see her big white-trimmed house in the distance. She relaxed, slowing to a normal walk.

Stirling checked behind them one more time, and then he breathed a sigh of relief. "Phew! That was close!" he exclaimed.

Kit decided to look on the bright side. "We got away—and they didn't steal your money," she pointed out. "And you only have two more weeks till school starts. Then you won't be selling newspapers in the afternoon anymore."

"Yeah," Stirling agreed. "If I can last two weeks, I'll be all right. But if they take all my money again—" He sank his hands deep into his pockets and was silent.

Kit knew that Stirling needed the money he was earning. Stirling and his mother, Mrs. Howard, were boarding with the Kittredge family. Mrs. Howard had been able to find only part-time work, and now she was away caring for her sick sister in Cleveland. Stirling was determined to save up money so that he could give it to his mother when she returned home.

"Maybe you should go to the police," suggested Kit. "They could make the bullies stop bothering you."

"Vinnie already tried that," said Stirling, sounding glum. "But the policeman said he needed proof, and Vinnie didn't even know the kids' names."

"Who's Vinnie?" asked Kit.

"He's another newspaper boy who works in the neighborhood. He sells your paper, the *Register*. He's just a little kid, but he's good at selling papers. Or at least he was, till the bullies started stealing from him." Stirling shook his head. "It's hopeless."

"Well, Mrs. Maggiano called them the Hobart brothers, so at least we know their last name now," said Kit, trying to cheer him up. "And I'll stand watch for you whenever I can. But we have to hurry—I have chores to do before we can leave for the play."

Kit and Stirling quickened their pace again.

A Job to Do

As they got closer to the house, Kit could see the neat rows of beans, tomatoes, and other vegetables growing in the backyard. Before the Depression, colorful flowers had bloomed throughout the yard, but now the backyard was used to grow food.

"Waste not, want not," Kit's Aunt Millie always said, and the Kittredge family tried not to waste anything. Because of the Depression, Kit's dad had lost his job, and for a long time he hadn't been able to find more work. To pay their bills, the Kittredges had decided to rent rooms in their house to boarders. Stirling and his mother had one room; Mrs. Dalrymple, a widow, and Miss Jemison, a nurse, occupied another room.

Kit's eighteen-year-old brother, Charlie, usually shared the sleeping porch with Mr. Peck, a musician who played the bass fiddle. But Charlie was working out west this summer. So Mr. Peck was sharing the sleeping porch with Mr. Bell, an elderly widowed actor who had stayed with the Kittredges in the past. Mr. Bell had come back to Cincinnati with the company of actors now performing at the Burns Theater.

As Kit and Stirling walked up to the house, they met Mr. Bell walking out. The white-haired actor always wore a suit and a dapper bow tie—even on the hottest days—and he had old-fashioned manners, too. He tipped his straw hat to Kit and Stirling. "I'm off to the theater," he said with a smile. "I shall see you there."

"We're looking forward to it!" exclaimed Kit.

"And good luck tonight!" Stirling added.

The old man's smile faded. "In the theater, you never wish an actor good luck," he explained gently. "Instead, you say, 'Break a leg.' It's rather a silly superstition, I suppose, but it *is* a tradition."

"Well, break a leg, then!" declared Kit.

"Thank you," said Mr. Bell. He tipped his hat again and continued down the path.

When Kit entered the house, her mother

called to her from the kitchen. "Ruthie came by about an hour ago and dropped off Felix," Mrs. Kittredge said. "She was leaving for her grandparents' house and said to say good-bye to you."

I forgot about Felix! Kit realized. Felix was a goldfish who belonged to Kit's best friend, Ruthie. Kit had promised to feed him while Ruthie was away visiting her grandparents.

Kit ran up the two flights of stairs to her attic room. On her desk, she found Felix swimming inside a large fishbowl that Ruthie had lovingly decorated with plants, colorful rocks, and a tiny model of a sunken ship. Next to the fishbowl, there was a jar labeled "Fish Food" and a note:

Dear Kit,

Thank you for taking care of Felix. I hope he won't be too much trouble. Please give him a tiny pinch of fish food once a day. I'll see you in a week!

Your friend,
Ruthie

*P.S. If you meet Daphne Dumont tonight,
would you PLEASE get her autograph
for my collection? I don't have the auto-
graphs of any actresses yet!*

P.P.S. Don't forget to write!!!

As Kit put down Ruthie's note, she felt
a twinge of envy. For the next week, Ruthie
would be swimming, boating, and playing
with her cousins at her grandparents' lakeside
cottage. Kit wished *she* could dive into a nice
cool lake right now, but instead she had to do
her boring old chores.

"At least *you* get to swim as much as you
want, right, Felix?" Kit said to the little fish.
"And tonight I'm going to see a play—and I'll
write my best column ever."

Glancing at Ruthie's note again, Kit suddenly had an idea. Daphne Dumont was
starring in *A Midsummer Night's Dream*, and
Kit decided that she'd ask Miss Dumont for
an autograph *and* an interview. Kit smiled

at the thought of how impressed her editor, Mr. Gibson, would be if she interviewed the star of the show.

If this interview goes well, maybe Mr. Gibson will let me interview the mayor someday, Kit told herself. *Or maybe even the governor. Or . . .*

Kit's happy dreams were interrupted by her mother's voice. "Kit! Time to set the table for dinner!" Kit quickly put on her best summer outfit—a short-sleeved dress with pink and red flowers and red shoes that her mother had found for her in a secondhand store. Then she grabbed her pencil and notebook and hurried downstairs to dinner.

One of Kit's chores was to help wash the dinner dishes. But as soon as dinner was finished, Aunt Millie picked up the dishcloth. "I'll help in the kitchen tonight," she said firmly. "You and Stirling go along now and get to the theater early."

Aunt Millie was a former schoolteacher, and she was as excited about Kit seeing the play as Kit herself was. "Shakespeare's wonderful,"

Aunt Millie declared. "And I don't want you to miss a single minute of the play."

"Yes," Kit's mother agreed. "But it'll be late when the show is over, so walk home with Mr. Bell."

Kit gratefully accepted Aunt Millie's offer, and she and Stirling set out for the theater. Their route took them through the neighborhood where Stirling sold newspapers. As they passed Maggiano's Grocery Store, Stirling looked around uneasily. But the stores were closed now and the streets were quiet. Only a few people were strolling down the sidewalk, and none of them looked like the Hobart brothers.

The Burns Theater was set across the street from a small city park dotted with maple, dogwood, and magnolia trees. To reach the theater, Kit and Stirling had to walk past the tree-shaded park. The evening was still hot, and Kit was grateful for the light breeze that rustled the magnolia leaves and cooled her flushed face.

She and Stirling were less than a block from the theater when Stirling stopped abruptly. "It's them!" he exclaimed, his voice little more than a whisper.

Kit looked up and saw the three blond boys approaching. Her heart began to pound. She and Stirling would have to pass the boys to get to the theater. What if the bullies demanded money?

Kit had carefully hidden her dollar bill in her shoe. It was the only money she had, and she needed it to buy tickets for the play.

If the bullies take my money, she thought, *I'll never get to see the show!*

2

A SURPRISE ANNOUNCEMENT

The three bullies were talking loudly
as they swaggered down the sidewalk. The
tallest brother said something. Kit heard the
other boys laugh like donkeys. "Hee-haw,
hee-haw!"

They even sound mean! she thought as the
bullies came closer. The boys were walking
faster now.

"We've got to get out of here," Stirling
whispered.

Kit nodded, and looked desperately for an
escape. The Burns Theater stood just beyond
the bullies. People were trickling into the
theater through the open glass doors, and Kit
saw a motorcar pull up in front of the building.
A man in a gray suit stepped out of the car and

several children tumbled out after him. For a moment, the man reminded Kit of her father.

If only Dad were here right now, she thought. *Then those bullies wouldn't dare bother us!*

Suddenly, Kit realized that the bullies had no idea what her father looked like. If she could trick them into thinking that the man in the gray suit really *was* her father, she and Stirling might have a chance.

The three bullies were now so close that Kit could see them clearly. They all had white-blond hair and narrow eyes set in chubby, freckled faces. And they were all grinning nastily.

Kit touched Stirling's elbow. "Come on!" she whispered urgently. Then she looked past the bullies and toward the man in the suit. Waving her hand wildly, she started running and shouting, "Dad! Dad! Wait up!"

As Kit and Stirling sprinted past the brothers, Kit saw the bullies' looks of surprise and open-mouthed disappointment. A minute later, she and Stirling safely reached the lighted sidewalk in front of the theater. They walked quickly past the man in the gray suit, pretending not to notice his puzzled expression.

The Burns Theater was a tall building with stately white columns in the front. The building must have once looked elegant, but as Kit climbed the marble steps in front, she noticed that the columns were peeling now and needed a fresh coat of white paint. Inside the theater's glass doors, she stepped into a wide lobby with gold-framed mirrors and red carpeting. Some of the gilt had chipped off the mirrors, and the carpet was a bit worn, but the entrance was still impressive.

The lobby was filled with families dressed up for a night at the theater. The Burns Theater was offering a special tonight: adults who bought two-dollar tickets could buy children's tickets for fifty cents. Kit and Stirling joined the line for the box office. They stood behind a woman who smelled of lavender perfume and wore a lavender-colored dress. The woman's daughter kept tugging at her mother's hand

and asking, "When's the play going to start, Mama?"

As they waited in line, Kit pulled out her dollar bill and unfolded it. It was an old creased bill with a torn corner, and now part of it had turned pink from rubbing against her red shoe. Kit eyed the bill regretfully. She had been saving this dollar for a long time, and she was sorry she had to spend it.

Stirling saw the look on her face and frowned. "If it costs too much to buy my ticket—" he began hesitantly.

"We have a deal, remember?" Kit said. She had offered to buy Stirling's ticket if he'd come to the play with her and draw a picture to go with her article. Stirling was a good artist, and Kit knew that the newspaper always liked illustrations to go with the articles. "If I sell the article, I'll earn two dollars," she reminded him.

Stirling brightened. "I guess that would be a good deal," he said, and they inched forward in the line.

After about ten minutes, they reached the box office window. Mr. Bell was standing inside the small, glass-enclosed booth, and Kit handed him her dollar bill through a window-like opening. "Two tickets, please," she said.

Mr. Bell nodded, pretending not to recognize her. Children were supposed to be accompanied by a parent paying full price, but Mr. Bell had offered to make an exception for Kit and Stirling. "As a member of the cast, I have privileges," he had explained. "Still, it would be best not to let others in line know that you are getting special treatment."

So now he just handed Stirling and Kit two tickets. "I hope you enjoy the performance," he said formally.

Inside the theater, an usher directed Kit and Stirling to their seats, about halfway from the stage. Looking around the lavishly decorated theater, Kit saw that above the floor where she and Stirling were sitting, there were balcony and box seats upstairs. But most of the seats were empty.

A Surprise Announcement

"Not many people here," said Stirling, looking around. "Even with the fifty-cent special."

"Maybe more people will come soon," Kit suggested. A few more people filtered in before the play began, but not nearly enough to fill the big theater.

At exactly seven-thirty, the theater's lights dimmed. Then the heavy red velvet stage curtain rose. "Oooooh!" murmured the audience as the opening curtain revealed a royal palace surrounded by lush, colorful flower gardens.

As the play progressed, Kit leaned forward in her seat trying to catch every word the actors said. She watched in awe as the fairy queen danced onto the stage. She sighed as the beautiful Helena tried to win the love of Demetrius. She smiled when she saw Mr. Bell playing the role of a stern father. And she laughed out loud at the pranks of the fairies.

During the show's intermission, Kit and Stirling stepped outside for some fresh air, but then they hurried back into the theater. "I don't want to miss a single moment," Kit said as they settled into their seats. "I have to see what happens next."

When the curtain fell on the play's final act, Kit sat for a moment, silent. She felt as if she'd been visiting the fairy kingdom, and then been abruptly sent back to Earth. The audience began to applaud. "That was the most wonderful thing I've ever seen!" exclaimed Kit. She stood up and clapped so hard that the palms of her hands tingled.

"It *was* good," agreed Stirling, speaking loudly to be heard above the applause. "But I wish they'd talked in regular English."

The curtain opened again, and the cast bowed. As the applause died down and the audience took their seats again, a petite, red-haired young woman came out on the stage. Kit recognized her as the actress who had played one of the fairies. The woman was now dressed in a black business suit, and she introduced herself as Rose Burns, owner and manager of the theater.

"I'd like to announce a schedule change,"

Miss Burns said, smiling. "We'd originally planned to perform three more weeks of *A Midsummer Night's Dream,* but this is the closing night of the play."

Oh no! thought Kit. She stared down at her reporter's notebook. Her article for the children's page was due next week. But Mr. Gibson, the editor at the *Cincinnati Register,* wanted only the latest news. If *A Midsummer Night's Dream* was no longer being performed, Kit was sure that Mr. Gibson wouldn't want an article about it.

I'll have to write about something else, Kit realized. *But what?*

Miss Burns was still smiling. "Instead, we're going to present one of Shakespeare's most exciting plays. It's a tragedy complete with a ghost, sword fights, and witches."

Kit saw the lead actors stare at Miss Burns in surprise.

"Because of old superstitions about this tragedy, some actors believe that it's bad luck to say the play's name inside the theater.

Instead, they call it 'the Scottish play' or even just 'the play,'" Miss Burns continued. Then she paused dramatically.

Kit noticed that several of the cast members were looking at each other. Some were frowning. *They aren't happy about the change in plans either,* she realized.

"But we're proud to announce that next week we'll be performing"—Miss Burns paused slightly again—"*Macbeth!* We hope you'll attend. Thank you, and good night."

The heavy red velvet curtain slowly closed, and the stage lights faded. The audience started to rustle in their seats. But before the house lights came up again, there was a thundering crash from behind the curtain.

3
STOLEN!

For a moment, Kit sat in stunned silence. She heard a scream from backstage. Then all around her in the dimly lit theater, she heard people asking, "What was that?" "What happened?"

Kit remembered that Mr. Bell had been behind the curtain with the rest of the cast. "I hope Mr. Bell's all right," Stirling said in a low voice.

"Me, too," Kit agreed.

A dark-haired young man suddenly burst from behind the curtain. "Is there a doctor in the house?" he yelled to the audience.

"I'm a doctor," an elderly man in the front row replied. He hurried onto the stage and was ushered behind the velvet curtain. Just as the curtain was closing again, a stout man in a wrinkled suit ran up to the stage and followed the doctor backstage.

A few moments later, the young, dark-haired man appeared again. "There was just a slight accident," he explained to the audience. "There's nothing to be concerned about. Please exit at the back of the theater."

Although the man's words were reassuring, he seemed worried. The house lights came on, and audience members began to leave the theater quickly, as if eager to get away.

Kit and Stirling hurried outside and around to the back of the theater, where Mr. Bell had told them to meet him after the show. They climbed up a short flight of outside stairs that led to a heavy door. Just as they were about to knock on the door, a dark-haired man swung it open. It was the same man who had made the announcements onstage. He stopped short when he saw Kit and Stirling on the landing. "What do you want?" he demanded.

"We're looking for Mr. Bell," Kit explained.

"He's onstage," the man said. With a jerk of his head, the man motioned toward the room behind him. Then he brushed past Kit and Stirling and ran down the outside stairs.

Kit grabbed the door as it started to close, and she and Stirling stepped inside. They found themselves in a large, crowded room with walls painted a sickly shade of green. Several doors opened off the room like spokes on a wheel. There was a smell of burnt coffee, and Kit saw a table and a coffee percolator at one end of the room. At the other end of the room, "Stage Door" was painted in fading letters on a wooden door.

Stirling said something to Kit, but the room was so noisy, she couldn't understand him. Actors were loudly talking and arguing. In one corner, a young actress was crying as the doctor examined her ankle. Near the doctor, the stout man in the rumpled suit was firing questions at Miss Burns and jotting down her answers on a notepad.

I bet he's a reporter, Kit thought. *I wonder what's happened?*

Together, she and Stirling threaded their way through the crowded room toward the stage door. The door was partly open, and Kit saw that it led to a short stairway. After a moment's hesitation, she and Stirling climbed the stairs. As they approached the stage from the back, Kit could see heavy ropes and pulleys hanging down from the ceiling and a confusing number of switches on the wall. A handwritten sign above the switches warned: DO NOT TOUCH!

The theater looks so different from this side of the curtain, Kit realized. *It's like a whole other world!*

When Kit stepped out onto the stage, she was startled to find broken pieces of wood and flattened flower garlands littering the stage. Mr. Bell was one of several men picking up pieces of the wreckage.

"I'm glad you found me," Mr. Bell greeted them with a smile. Then he saw the concerned looks on Kit's and Stirling's faces. "I hope you weren't worried. This arch was part of the fairy kingdom's scenery. It collapsed just after the curtain closed. Luckily, no one was hurt."

"What about the scream?" asked Stirling. "And the doctor?"

"One of the actresses twisted her ankle as she ran offstage," Mr. Bell explained. "I think she'll be fine, though."

Kit breathed a sigh of relief. Then she told Mr. Bell that a reporter was asking Miss Burns questions about the accident.

A shadow crossed Mr. Bell's face. "Oh dear," he said, half to himself. "I hope there won't be stories about it in the newspaper. If the Scottish play is going to succeed, we'll need good publicity, not bad."

Kit nodded. She thought about everything she'd seen backstage, and she suddenly had an idea. "Could I talk to Miss Burns?" she asked Mr. Bell. "Maybe I could write my column about *Macbeth*."

Mr. Bell winced at the sound of *Macbeth.* "You really shouldn't say that word in the theater," he cautioned. "Some actors believe that it brings bad luck. Call it 'the Scottish play' instead."

"What if someone says *Mac*—" Stirling caught himself just in time. "I mean, the play's real name by mistake?" he asked.

"Well, one remedy is to go outside and turn around three times and then spit on the ground to reverse the curse," Mr. Bell advised. The dignified old man spoke matter-of-factly, as if he were telling Stirling where to catch a bus or how to find the post office.

Does he really believe in curses? Kit wondered.

Then Mr. Bell smiled. "Of course, it's just a superstition," he said. "But it *is* a theater tradition." He turned to Kit. "Now, if you'd like to talk with Miss Burns, come with me."

Mr. Bell led them from the front of the stage, through the theater aisles, and into the elegant lobby. He pointed to a half-glass door at the far end of the lobby past the box office.

"When you're finished, look for me. I'll either be onstage or in the box office."

Kit and Stirling crossed the red carpet to the theater manager's office. Kit clutched her reporter's notebook tightly and then knocked on the door. There was a loud yapping from within.

"Don't mind Dionysius," a young woman's voice sounded from behind them. "He was my father's dog, and he barks at everyone he doesn't know."

Kit turned and saw Miss Burns walking quickly toward them through the lobby. The theater manager looked smaller and younger than she had onstage. Even though she was wearing high heels, she was only a little taller than Kit herself, and she didn't look much older than Kit's brother, Charlie.

Miss Burns opened the door to her office, scooped up a white terrier, and put the dog out in the lobby. "Come on in," she told Kit and Stirling as she switched on the overhead light.

Miss Burns sat down in the swivel chair

behind her desk. She motioned Kit and Stirling toward the two straight chairs on the other side of the desk. "You're awfully young to be looking for jobs, aren't you?" she asked. "Besides, I'm not hiring for *Macbeth* till Tuesday."

"We're not looking for work," Kit told her. "Well, not exactly, anyway."

Kit and Stirling introduced themselves, and Kit explained that she wrote a children's column for the *Cincinnati Register*. "I was hoping I could come to the rehearsals for *Macbeth*," she told the manager. "I want to write about the play for my next column."

Miss Burns looked doubtful. "*Macbeth* isn't a comedy like *A Midsummer Night's Dream*," she warned. "It's a great play, but it's a tragedy and it's very scary. Do you really think children would want to read about it?"

Kit swallowed hard. "My idea is to write about *how* a play is made and what happens backstage—the scenery, the actors, everything," she explained to Miss Burns. "I'd never been to a real play before tonight, and I bet a lot of other kids haven't either. They'll want to know all about it."

"It *might* work," the manager said thoughtfully. She picked up a folder of papers from her desk and headed for the door. "Wait here. I'll be right back," she said, and she closed the door behind her.

Kit and Stirling looked around the office. It smelled faintly of pipe smoke, and it was cluttered with books, papers, and all sorts of memorabilia. In one corner of the room, there was an old icebox with a sign that said, "Important! Keep door closed in case of fire!"

But the door was hanging ajar, and Kit could see that, instead of being filled with food, the shelves of the icebox were crammed with red leather-bound books. "I wonder why Miss Burns keeps books in an icebox," Kit whispered to Stirling.

"I bet this was her dad's office," Stirling suggested. "Look over there." He pointed to the framed photos on the walls. Many of them included a small, mischievous-looking old man smiling as he posed with actors and actresses.

Kit was studying the photos when she heard Miss Burns's voice in the lobby. "I don't care how my father *used* to do it," Miss Burns was saying. "I'm the manager of the theater now, and *I'll* decide how we put on the play."

Miss Burns came into the office with the tall, dark-haired man who had been on the back steps of the theater. She introduced the man as Graham Walker, assistant manager of the theater, and she told Kit and Stirling to call her Rose. "We're not very formal in the theater," she said, smiling as she sat down behind her desk again.

Graham nodded agreement, but there wasn't a hint of a smile on his face. He stood near the door, his arms crossed. He had a serious, commanding air, and, in the light of the office, Kit could see that a thin white scar ran down his left cheek.

Graham took one look at Kit and shook his head. "We don't need any girls for *Macbeth*," he told her. "There's only one child's part, and it's for a boy." He looked at Stirling. "As for you..."

"But I'm not here for a—" Stirling began to protest.

"Sorry," Graham dismissed him. "We need a *young* boy. Your voice is too big for the role."

Stirling, who was always being told that he was too small, flushed with pride. Kit finally had a chance to explain that she wanted to write a children's column about the play, and Stirling was going to help by drawing illustrations.

"You and your friend will have to find something else to write about," Graham said abruptly. "We can't have kids hanging around the theater all the time."

Kit's hopes fell. *What will I write about?* she worried, looking down at the blank pages of her notebook.

Then Rose stood up. "Actually, I think a children's column would be an excellent idea."

"What?" Graham demanded.

Miss Burns turned to him. "Tonight we had a reporter here from the *Cincinnati Daily Herald.* He was asking me all sorts of questions about the *Macbeth* jinx and whether it was responsible for tonight's accident. What the Burns Theater could use is some *good* publicity. A column on the children's page would be perfect."

Graham's face tightened. "You're the boss," he told Rose. "I just hope you know what you're doing." Then he stalked out of the office, closing the door so hard that the pane of frosted glass in the top shivered.

After Graham left, Rose settled back in her chair. "We have a lot to do to get ready for *Macbeth,*" she said briskly. "So if you're here working on your article, we may ask you to help out from time to time—painting backdrops, helping to clean up, that sort of thing."

"I don't mind doing chores," Kit said. "I do them all the time at home."

"Good," said Rose. "Because we're going to be awfully busy. First, we'll have to hire the actors we'll need."

"Don't you already have a lot of actors?" asked Stirling.

Rose explained that the Burns Theater had hired a company of actors for the month of August. The stars of the company were two established actors from New York: Daphne Dumont and Roland Fairchild. The other members included Cecilia Smith, who was a young actress from Canada, and two Swedish brothers, Gunnar and Sven, who used to be circus strongmen. Mr. Bell, who had worked in the Burns Theater in the past, had joined the company in Chicago. He performed small roles and took charge of the box office.

The actors were all skilled professionals, and they knew several Shakespeare plays, including *Macbeth*. They had performed the plays so many times in the past that they could open a new show in a new city with only a few days' rehearsal. The actors in the company performed the main characters' roles in the plays, while local actors were hired for smaller roles. Rose and Graham also took on roles as needed.

"We'll hire some local people for *Macbeth*," said Rose. "We'll need a young boy, five or six soldiers, and at least two witches."

Witches! Kit thought. She and Stirling shared an uneasy glance.

"Some of the women who play witches could double as soldiers, too—as long as we put them in suits of armor and they don't have to say anything," Rose continued, as if speaking to herself.

"So people can play more than one role in the play?" asked Kit, writing notes as fast as she could.

"Oh yes," said Rose. "We'll save money that way." She looked at Kit's notebook. "I hope you won't mention this in your article, but we're a bit short of money right now. You see, my father ran this theater for years, but he died a few months ago."

Kit put down her notebook. "Oh," she said. "I'm sorry."

Stirling, whose own father had disappeared three years ago, looked down at the floor and murmured his sympathy.

"Thank you," said Rose. She explained that her parents had separated when she was a small child. Rose had grown up living with her mother, who was an actress in New York. "I really didn't know my father very well. When I heard he was ill, I rushed back here to see him. But I was too late."

She was silent for a moment, and then she looked around the crowded office. "This theater was my father's life. I've been trying my best to keep it going, but it isn't easy. We had to close *A Midsummer Night's Dream* because we were losing money—even when we offered fifty-cent tickets for children we didn't fill the theater."

"A lot of parents can't afford two-dollar tickets," said Kit, thinking of her own parents.

"I know. But we have to sell tickets, or we'll go out of business," Rose said, glancing at the bills on her desk. "My father always said that audiences love *Macbeth*. I hope he was right— we need a success if we're going to survive."

Just then there was an agitated knock on the office door. Without waiting for a response, Mr. Bell entered. His face was the color of gray-white smoke. "Someone," he burst out, "has stolen all the cash from the box office."

4

DESPERATE ACTS

"There's got to be some mistake!" Rose
exclaimed. She jumped up from her chair
and rushed across the lobby to the small,
glassed-in box office. Mr. Bell, Kit, and
Stirling followed close behind. Dionysius
trotted eagerly at their heels.

Kit heard Mr. Bell's voice shake as he
explained to Rose that he had bolted the
theater's glass front doors after all the audience had left. Then he had counted all the
money in the box office and put it away in
the cash drawer.

"What happened next?" asked Rose, her
forehead creased with worry.

"I was rather tired," Mr. Bell confessed.
"So while Kit and Stirling were talking with

you in your office, I went backstage to get a cup of coffee. I locked the cash drawer, but—"

Mr. Bell hesitated, passing a weary hand over his eyes. "But I foolishly left the key there," he continued, pointing to a ring of keys hanging on a hook at the back of the box office. "I was away for perhaps ten minutes. When I came back to the lobby, I saw a young man hurrying down the front steps, away from the theater. At first, I thought nothing of it. Then I decided to check the front door, and I found that someone had unbolted it from the inside. When I picked up the cash box, I discovered this—"

Mr. Bell showed them a wooden box divided into compartments. The box held plenty of quarters, dimes, nickels, and pennies, but there were empty spaces where the bills should have been.

Rose looked down at the vacant compartments. "How much is missing?"

"About one hundred and fifty dollars,"

Mr. Bell said. His hands trembled slightly
as he put the box away.

That's an awful lot of money! thought Kit.
"Shouldn't we call the police?" she asked.

"Not yet," Rose said quickly. "The theater
can't afford any more bad publicity." She
turned to Mr. Bell. "What did the thief look
like?"

Mr. Bell shook his head. "I'm afraid I
didn't get a good look at him," he admitted.
He paused, screwing up his face as if he was
trying to remember every detail. "He was
tall and thin. He wore a dark-colored jacket
and a cap pulled over his face. By the way he
walked, I'd guess he was fairly young."

Rose took a deep breath. "Let's call everyone together," she said. "Maybe somebody
saw the thief."

A few minutes later, Kit and Stirling were
sitting in the wings of the theater as the cast
members gathered on the stage. The local
actors who had been hired only for *A Midsummer Night's Dream* had gone home, but the

members of the acting company were still in the theater. Kit looked closely at the stars. She decided that Roland Fairchild was handsome, but in person he looked much older than he had onstage. Daphne Dumont was beautiful even without stage makeup. She was tall and slender with long auburn hair, fair skin, and doe-like hazel eyes—but she, too, looked older than she had onstage.

Kit recognized Cecilia Smith as the pretty, slightly plump young woman who had twisted her ankle; it was now wrapped in a bandage. Both Sven and Gunnar were big, heavily muscled men. Gunnar spoke quietly, and he had a gentle, almost shy smile. Sven, however, had a booming voice. When Rose announced the theft, Sven threw down the scenery he was carrying and shouted something in a foreign language.

Rose began questioning the cast. After about half an hour, it became clear that no one had seen anyone resembling the thief. Both the women had been in their dressing rooms or in the central area they called the "greenroom." The men had all been working around the stage, carrying sets to the theater's basement and costumes and props to the attic.

Roland Fairchild suggested that an outsider had probably sneaked into the theater and stolen the money. Rose agreed that was a possibility, but she pointed out that the thief hadn't had much time, and an outsider wouldn't have known where to look for the key to the cash drawer. Also, Dionysius had been in the lobby, and he would have barked if a stranger had come in.

"Did you hear the dog bark?" Kit asked Stirling in a whisper.

"No," Stirling whispered back. "Did you?"

Kit shook her head. She had an uneasy feeling in her stomach. *The thief must be someone in the theater,* she thought. *But who?*

Sven spoke up. He had a slight Swedish accent that Kit hadn't noticed when he'd been onstage. "You know, we only have Bell's word that it was a tall young man."

Kit saw the pained expression that passed over Mr. Bell's face. She jumped to her feet. "Mr. Bell would never lie!" she burst out.

In the awkward silence that followed, Kit was suddenly aware that all the cast members were staring at her. Mr. Bell looked even more uncomfortable.

"What're those kids doing here?" Roland asked.

In a flat voice, Graham explained that Kit was doing an article on the theater and Stirling was going to illustrate it. His tone made it clear that he disapproved of the whole idea.

"A kid reporter hanging around the theater?" exclaimed Sven. He shouted something else in Swedish. Then he threw up his hands in disgust and walked off the stage.

"You must excuse my brother," Gunnar told the others. "I think he is tired. It has been a long day, and this..." Gunnar hesitated. "Well, it is a disappointment."

"We all need some sleep," Rose announced. "We'll talk more tomorrow, but in the meantime let's keep this theft to ourselves." She looked pointedly at Kit. "The last thing we need is more bad publicity about the theater."

It was late by the time Kit and Stirling walked home with Mr. Bell, and the night air felt damp. Stirling kept looking around the dark city streets, alert for any sign of the bullies. Mr. Bell, however, seemed lost in thought. "How could I have been so careless?" he muttered to himself.

Kit wished she could think of some way to help Mr. Bell. Then she remembered that, as a reporter, she'd have a chance to go to the theater every day and ask questions. *Maybe,* she thought, *I can find out who the thief really is!*

5

JINXED?

The next morning, Kit woke up to the tantalizing smell of pancakes. The sun was shining hard into her attic bedroom and the heat was stifling. Kit realized that she'd slept late—and she was very hungry. As she threw on her clothes, she noticed Felix. The little fish was in the corner of his bowl, popping his head out of the water.

"I guess you're ready for your breakfast, too," said Kit as she sprinkled a tiny pinch of food into the water. But Felix didn't seem interested in the food flakes. He was swimming listlessly and poking his head out, as if he were gasping for air. As Kit watched him, she became increasingly worried.

Is something wrong? she wondered. *Should*

JINXED?

I have fed him last night instead?

She carried the bowl downstairs to the kitchen, where Aunt Millie was cleaning up after breakfast. "Do you think he's sick?" Kit asked.

Aunt Millie watched the fish for a few minutes. "Maybe he's just trying to cool down," she said finally. "Your room's pretty warm, isn't it?"

Kit nodded. The attic *was* hot. Kit's fan blew a cooling breeze on her bed, but it didn't reach the desk, where Felix's bowl had been.

"Why don't you put Felix in the living room?" Aunt Millie suggested. "It's the coolest room in the house. I'm sure your mother won't mind having him there. He'll be the newest— and the smallest—boarder."

Aunt Millie helped Kit settle the fishbowl on a table in the corner of the living room. "Now, come on into the kitchen," she told Kit. "Everyone else has already eaten, but I'll fry you up some pancakes, and you can tell me all about the play."

Kit sat down to a tall glass of milk and a stack of pancakes topped with Aunt Millie's homemade strawberry syrup. As Kit ate, she told Aunt Millie everything that had happened the previous evening. When she came to the theft, though, she hesitated. "Can you keep a secret?" Kit asked.

"Cross my heart," Aunt Millie promised.

So Kit described how Mr. Bell had discovered that money had been stolen from the box office. When Kit finished, Aunt Millie shook her head. "Poor Mr. Bell! No wonder he was looking so worn out this morning. He hardly touched his breakfast."

"I hope he doesn't feel too bad," said Kit, who had managed to finish her entire breakfast. "He just left the box office for a few minutes—it wasn't his fault someone stole the money."

Aunt Millie patted Kit's hand reassuringly. "Of course, it wasn't his fault," she agreed. "But he may feel responsible anyway. I just hope he doesn't lose his job."

Jinxed?

It hadn't occurred to Kit that Mr. Bell might lose his job over the theft. For a moment, she sat at the table staring at her empty milk glass. She knew that Mr. Bell had very little money and, since his wife's death last year, he had no family. The theater was his whole life.

What if he's fired for being careless? thought Kit, twisting her napkin in her hands. *What will he do?*

Just then, the screen door slammed and Stirling came into the kitchen. He'd been up early selling the morning edition of the *Cincinnati Daily Herald* and he carried a copy of the paper in his hand. He looked hot and dusty, and his newspaper bag hung empty from his shoulder.

"I'm sorry I wasn't up in time to go with you this morning," Kit told him.

"That's okay," said Stirling. "I met up with Vinnie—he was out selling the *Register*—and we worked the same corner so we could watch for the bullies together. I sold all my papers except this one." He gestured to the rolled-up paper in his hand. "I wanted to show it to you." Stirling opened the paper and spread it out on the kitchen table. Then he pointed to an article on page five. "Look at this!"

Aunt Millie and Kit read the article together. It was titled "Trick or Threat?" and it described the previous night's accident at the Burns Theater. Kit frowned as she read:

A crash behind the stage sounded as if the roof had fallen in. The audience was terrified. Screams echoed throughout the theater.

Kit looked up from the paper. "I wasn't exactly 'terrified,'" she said. "Were you?"

"No," said Stirling. "And I only heard one scream, and that was from the girl who twisted her ankle. I guess the reporter is trying to make it sound exciting."

Hmmm, thought Kit. *A good reporter should be exciting **and** accurate.* Then she continued reading. The reporter questioned whether last night's accident might be linked to the *Macbeth* jinx.

The superstition started in the 1600's, when the play was first performed. The actor who was supposed to play Lady Macbeth is said to have died, and Shakespeare himself took his place.

"Shakespeare was a man—how could he play the part of Lady Macbeth?" Kit asked.

"In Shakespeare's time, it wasn't considered proper for women to act on the stage, so men and boys played all the roles," Aunt Millie explained. "Even today, men sometimes play women's parts—and women occasionally play men's parts, too."

Stirling shuddered. "I'd *hate* having to pretend to be a girl."

"Well, *I'd* hate pretending to be a boy," said Kit, glaring at him. Then she returned to the article:

**During the early performances,
audiences feared that the witches onstage
were chanting evil spells. Since that time,
there have been rumors that the play is
jinxed. Over the last three hundred years,
a surprising number of actors have been
injured or have died during the play's
performance, and theaters have suffered
many accidents and fires.**

"This stuff really *is* scary," said Stirling as
he reread the article over Kit's shoulder.

Aunt Millie started to clear off the kitchen
table. "I wouldn't put much stock in it," she
said briskly. "Remember what Shakespeare
said: 'The fault, dear Brutus, is not in our stars,
but in ourselves.'"

"What's that mean?" Kit asked.

"Well, I've always taken it to mean that
when things go wrong, there's usually a simple
human explanation for it," Aunt Millie said.
She paused for a moment, a stack of dirty
plates in her hands. "Besides, if actors died or

theaters burned down whenever *Macbeth* was performed, wouldn't people have stopped putting on the play?"

Stirling didn't look convinced. "Maybe the jinx is like the medicine the doctor gives you—sometimes it works and sometimes it doesn't," he suggested. "How do we know for sure?"

"It sounds like the reporter isn't sure himself," Kit said. She read the last paragraph of the article out loud:

> **The theater's previous owner, Ian Burns, was known for playing outlandish stunts to gain publicity for his plays. Now that his daughter has inherited the Burns Theater, is Miss Burns playing the same kind of tricks that her father did? Or is the theater truly threatened by the "Macbeth jinx"?**

Stirling folded up the newspaper. "Well, I hope *Macbeth* doesn't jinx the Burns Theater," he said.

"I guess we'll find out on Monday," said Kit, taking her dishes to the sink.

"On Monday?" Stirling echoed.

"I'm going to the theater first thing Monday morning, as soon as I finish my chores," Kit explained.

"Oh!" said Stirling.

"I was hoping you'd come too, so you could draw an illustration for my story," Kit continued. She looked over at her friend. He was staring down at the newspaper story.

"But if you don't want to go, I'll try taking pictures with my camera instead," Kit offered. "I'm just not sure there's enough light inside the theater."

Stirling hesitated. "I'll go," he said finally. "You helped me watch out for the bullies, so I guess I can help you watch out for the jinx." He sighed. "But the last thing I need now is more bad luck."

6
SUSPICION

It was hot and muggy outside, and the sky was threatening rain as Kit and Stirling headed to the theater on Monday morning. They walked quickly, keeping a careful lookout for the Hobart brothers. Both Kit and Stirling were relieved when they arrived at the theater without seeing the bullies.

Inside the theater, they found most of the cast members gathered on the stage. Two large fans were *flip-flipping* noisily at opposite ends of the stage, but the theater was still uncomfortably warm.

Everyone was busy working. At one end of the stage, Sven and Gunnar were building a piece of scenery that looked like a castle. Sven shouted something in Swedish when he dropped a piece of wood on his foot. At the other end of the stage, Roland, in the role of Macbeth, was rehearsing with Daphne, who was Lady Macbeth. Cecilia was standing nearby with a copy of the play in her hand, and she prompted the lead actors whenever they forgot their lines.

Mr. Bell and Graham were cutting out what looked like an endless forest of cardboard trees. Graham looked up when Kit and Stirling came in. "It's you again!" he said with a frown.

Kit gathered up her courage. "I was hoping to interview Rose for my article and—"

"Rose is busy in the office," Graham interjected. "But as long as you're here, you might as well make yourself useful. Can you draw?"

"Not as well as Stirling can," Kit admitted.

Graham's frown deepened. "I suppose you could paint a wall, couldn't you?"

"I guess so," said Kit. She gestured to her reporter's notebook. "But I'd like to do some interviews, too."

"Sure, sure," said Graham. "There'll be time for that later." Graham put Stirling to work drawing the outlines of more trees on cardboard. Then he handed Kit a brush and a bucket of paint and instructed her to paint the wooden walls of the castle a medieval-looking gray.

Kit carefully painted the plywood, trying to be as neat as possible. Several times, Graham told her that she had missed a spot, so Kit had to go over areas that she'd already covered. She was glad when Rose came onstage, with Dionysius following closely at her heels.

Rose was carrying a stack of envelopes. "Well, everyone, I tallied up our earnings for the week and I have your shares," she announced.

All the actors dropped what they were doing and circled around Rose. Sven was the first to look inside his envelope. "This is it?" he boomed at Rose. "Is this some kind of joke?"

Cecilia looked in her envelope. "It's a good thing I'm staying at my aunt's house," she said sadly. "Otherwise, I wouldn't even be able to buy food."

"Surely this can't be right," Roland protested when he looked inside his envelope. "This is less than half of what I usually earn."

"I realize it's not what you expected," Rose said. "It's not what any of us expected. But your contracts state that we'll all share the profits from the shows. And since the thief stole all that money Saturday night—well, there isn't much left over to share."

Mr. Bell cleared his throat and all the actors turned to look at him. He was the only one who hadn't claimed a pay envelope. He said in a low voice, "I deeply regret my carelessness that night. To make amends, I would like you all to have my share of the earnings this week."

There was a murmur of approval at this. "Since I'm in charge of the theater, I feel partly responsible for the theft," Rose added. "So I'm skipping my pay this week, too." She held up her hands. "I'm sorry—that's all I can do."

"It's awfully convenient that the money disappeared just before payday," Sven grumbled. "Maybe someone should ask about the kind of management they hire in this theater."

Graham turned on him. "What do you mean by that?"

Sven eyed Graham suspiciously. "Daphne told us about your jail record."

Graham shot a glance at Daphne. She shrugged her elegant shoulders. "Theater is a small world," she said. "Gossip gets around."

"I was talking with Roland and Gunnar last night," Sven continued. "We figure that the thief is some tall, thin guy who knew where the keys and the cash box were kept." Sven pointed at Dionysius, who had settled himself in a corner. "And since that dog didn't bark, the guy's not a stranger."

Sven folded his massive arms and stared straight at Graham, who was the only tall, thin man in the room.

"Are you accusing me?" Graham demanded. His face was flushed with anger.

"No one is accusing anyone of anything," snapped Rose. She stepped between Sven and Graham. "But what's this about a jail record?"

Graham looked around at the assembled actors. "It's true that I once spent some time in jail, but Mr. Burns knew all about my past and he trusted me. I'll never forget that he hired me when no one else would."

Turning back to Rose, Graham said, "Your father worked himself to death to keep this theater running. And if you think I'd ever steal a dime from it—" He paused. "Well, then you don't know much about your father or me."

For a moment everyone on the stage was silent. Kit studied Graham's face. He looked as if he was telling the truth, but Kit couldn't be sure.

Suddenly, Dionysius gave a low growl and jumped up. He ran backstage toward the greenroom, barking wildly. Rose lifted her eyebrows. "We're not expecting company, are we?" she asked Graham.

Graham shook his head, but he looked worried. Together, he and Rose hurried back-stage. Kit and Stirling and the rest of the cast followed them. As they entered the greenroom, Kit saw Dionysius barking ferociously by the back door. The door was bolted, but someone was pounding on it.

A man's voice could be heard above the barking. "Open up!" he shouted. "We have an order from the sheriff's department!"

Kit caught her breath. *What now?* she thought.

Rose started toward the door. "Don't let them in!" Graham called to her urgently. "Tell them to go to the front door. Then stall them as long as you can!"

Then Graham turned to the other actors. "Get everything we need for *Macbeth*. Hurry!" He turned to Kit and Stirling. "You two come with me," he said before they could ask any questions.

A Thief in the Theater

"We'll get Daphne's costumes first," Graham directed. He led the way to a private dressing room off the greenroom. It was a small room, painted pale pink, with a wide window that looked out on a fire escape. There was a vase of fresh flowers on the vanity table, and the whole room smelled of perfume.

Graham strode through the room, yanked open the closet door, and pulled out three costumes. "Hold these," he said, handing the long dresses to Kit.

The dresses were heavier than Kit had expected, and she had to bundle them up in her arms. Graham led her and Stirling to another, slightly smaller dressing room that smelled of cigars. There were no flowers in this room, but there was a large mirror. This was Roland's dressing room, and the star was already gathering up an armload of clothes from the closet. Graham picked up several wooden swords and shields and handed the props to Stirling.

"Come on!" Graham ordered, grabbing a suit of armor. He led Kit and Stirling to a closet off the greenroom.

"What are we doing?" said Kit. Peering over the heavy costumes in her arms, she saw Graham reach into the closet and push aside some hanging costumes. Then he opened up another door at the back of the closet.

"We're going up here," said Graham, carrying the armor up the stairs.

Kit and Stirling followed him. At the top of the stairs they found themselves in an attic with a high, pitched ceiling. A few round windows brought in light and air. On one side of the stairs, there was a neatly made bed, a wooden dresser, and a desk and chair. It reminded Kit of her attic bedroom at home.

Graham headed toward the other side of the stairs where trunks were surrounded by a broken birdcage, a cardboard replica of a grandfather clock, a giant witch's cauldron, and other props. Graham tossed the suit of armor onto a trunk. Then he took the items

Kit and Stirling were carrying and threw them onto trunks, too. "Thanks," he said. "Now get back to whatever you were doing onstage."

On their way downstairs, Kit and Stirling passed Cecilia, Mr. Bell, Sven, Gunnar, and Roland—all carrying more costumes and props to the attic.

Kit had just picked up her paintbrush again when a burly man in a black suit entered the theater. Rose was following the man and arguing with him every step of the way.

Graham strolled casually onto the stage. "What's the problem?" he asked.

Kit heard the man in the black suit explain that the Burns Theater owed money to the Stagecraft Supplies Company. Because the theater couldn't pay its bills, Stagecraft was reclaiming some of its property.

Graham protested, but the man from Stagecraft paid no attention. He called in two uniformed assistants and together they packed up more than a dozen boxes of costumes and props. Graham fought over each item they wanted to reclaim. "You're driving us out of business!" he shouted finally, the white scar on his cheek standing out against his tanned skin.

Kit tried to continue her painting, but she had a hard time keeping her mind on her work. *Will the theater still be able to go on?* she worried.

After the men took out the last box from the greenroom, Graham bolted the theater's doors. When he turned around, Kit was amazed to see that he was smiling. "At least they didn't get anything important," he said cheerfully.

"What about all those boxes?" Kit protested. "You seemed so angry!"

Graham laughed. "I had to make 'em *think* they were getting all the best stuff, didn't I?" he asked. "But Mr. Burns taught me that if collection guys come knocking at the door, the first thing you do is hide the important stuff in the attic. So now everything we need for the play is up there—safe and sound."

Graham walked back toward the stage,

whistling softly to himself. *He wasn't really angry at all,* Kit realized. *It was just an act!*

Then another thought occurred to her. *I wonder what else he's lying about?*

7

TOIL AND TROUBLE

When Kit opened her eyes on Tuesday
morning, her room was so warm that she
felt wilted even before she got out of bed.
I hope Felix is all right, she thought as she
pushed off her sheet and stood up in the
stifling heat.

She put on her coolest summer dress and
hurried down the two flights of stairs. As
she reached the main floor, she saw Stirling.
He was about to head out the door with his
newspaper bag. "I'll go with you," Kit offered.
"Just wait a minute while I check on Felix."

"It's okay," said Stirling, standing as tall as
he could. "You don't have to keep watch for
me anymore. I've been selling my papers with
Vinnie, and we found a corner where those

guys don't bother us. It's a little farther to walk but it's worth it."

"Can you still meet me at the theater?" Kit asked.

"I'll see you there when I'm done," he promised.

In the living room, Kit was relieved to find Felix swimming around his bowl. She fed him and then watched as he eagerly chased the flakes through the water.

Kit grinned. "Felix is fine now," she reported to Aunt Millie, who was sitting on the back porch, shucking corn. "Thank heavens! I would've felt terrible writing Ruthie that he was sick."

"It wouldn't have been your fault," said Aunt Millie. She pulled a tiny worm off a corncob and then tossed the shucked corn into a basket. "But sometimes we can feel poorly about something even if we're not really to blame."

"You're right," said Kit. She thought of Mr. Bell, who had looked so uncomfortable when Rose handed out the pay envelopes. She told Aunt Millie what had happened at the theater yesterday, and how she had started working on her column.

"I want to write about how actors put on a play, but I don't understand *Macbeth* at all," Kit complained. Sitting down beside Aunt Millie, she picked up an ear of corn and started shucking it. "Why are there witches?" she asked, ripping off the first layer of husk. "Who is the ghost?" She peeled off the second layer. "And is there really a forest that moves?"

Kit picked off the last shreds of corn silk and then tossed the golden ear into the basket. She turned to her aunt. "Can you tell me what happens in the play?"

"Margaret Mildred Kittredge, you've come to the right person!" exclaimed Aunt Millie, and the lines around her eyes crinkled as she smiled. "You know I love Shakespeare, and *Macbeth* is one of his greatest plays! I have a copy of it in my room—you and I can read it together."

"Me?" Kit questioned. She shook her head. "I don't know—there are all those *thee*'s and *thou*'s and words I don't understand."

"I'll help you," Aunt Millie promised. "But first, I'll give you a little bit of background." She picked up another ear of corn. "You see, *Macbeth* is about a man who desperately wants to be king. And desperate people sometimes do desperate things..."

By midmorning, Kit had finished her dusting, mopping, and other chores. She sat down with Aunt Millie, and together they read the opening scene of *Macbeth*. Kit was surprised to find that the first scene was short—only about a page long—and she got through it fairly easily.

The next scenes were longer and harder. Aunt Millie read parts out loud, acting out the voices and making each character sound different. Whenever Kit was confused, Aunt Millie stopped and explained what was happening.

When they'd finally finished Act One, Aunt Millie closed the book, promising they'd read more later.

Maybe I'll be able to understand this play after all, Kit thought. She picked up her reporter's notebook and headed for the Burns Theater. When she reached the park, she was surprised to see a crowd of people in front of the theater. Men and women were standing in a line that stretched down the steps and around toward the back of the theater.

"Excuse me," said Kit when she reached the front steps. "What's everybody waiting for?"

"A job," said a woman in a fashionable hat. "They're auditioning today for *Macbeth.* People started lining up hours ago. You'd better go to the back of the line."

A thin woman wearing bright red lipstick turned around. "Sorry, honey," she said. "But you'd be wasting your time to even try out. They don't have any parts for young girls."

"Oh, I'm not looking for a part," Kit explained. She gestured to the notebook in her hands. "I'm a reporter." Kit saw the looks of surprise on the women's faces. She felt like a real reporter as she edged her way to the head of the line.

Mr. Bell stood at the front door. He was telling the job-seekers that they had to be patient. When he caught sight of Kit, he let her slip into the theater, despite the grumblings of those in line.

"How many new actors are going to be hired?" Kit asked Mr. Bell after he had shut the glass doors and she was safely inside the lobby.

He glanced at the long line outside. "Probably nine or ten," he said. "And they'll just be temporary, not part of the regular company, so they'll only work as long as this play is running."

"Oh," said Kit, thinking of all those people waiting in the hot sun. "It's not easy to work in the theater, is it?"

"It's not easy to get a job anywhere these days—but the theater is probably one of the hardest places of all," said Mr. Bell. He smiled, but his blue eyes looked worried.

As soon as Kit reached the stage, Graham handed her a paintbrush and asked her to paint a large plywood partition solid black. "Don't miss any spots this time," he warned.

If he didn't like the way I painted the last wall, why is he asking me to paint another one? Kit wondered.

As she swished the black paint across the wood, Kit listened to Rose audition actresses for the witches' roles. One by one, the actresses recited the famous spell that the witches chanted over cauldrons: "Double, double toil and trouble; Fire burn and cauldron bubble."

Kit heard the spell repeated dozens of times, but each actress said the lines slightly differently. Some witches sounded angry, a few sounded old and withered, and still others spoke with a quiet intensity that was strangely frightening. *I bet it's hard to choose which witch would be best,* Kit thought.

When the partition she was painting was

finally an inky black, Graham told Kit she
could take a break. Kit decided to make the
most of her free time. She went backstage and,
with her notebook in her hand, knocked at
Daphne Dumont's dressing-room door.

"One moment, please," Daphne's lilting
voice came from within. There was a pause.
Then Daphne opened the door. She looked at
Kit curiously. "Yes?"

"I'm—I'm sorry to bother you, but could
you give me your autograph?" Kit stammered.
"My friend Ruthie asked me to get it for her."

"Of course," said Daphne graciously. Her
long auburn hair was twisted into a chignon,
and she was wearing a cream-colored silk
dress and a string of pearls. Despite the heat,
Daphne looked cool, sophisticated, and glam-
orous—just the way Kit had always imagined
a famous actress should look.

Kit followed the star into the perfume-
scented room. On the dressing table there
was a fresh bouquet of flowers along with a
pile of paperwork. Daphne took out a sheet

of monogrammed notepaper and, using a silver pen, wrote boldly across the page, *Daphne Dumont.*

Kit thanked her and slipped the paper between the pages of her notebook. Then she took out her pencil. "Also, could I interview you for my article? I have just a few questions I'd like to ask."

Daphne shook her head regretfully. "I'm afraid I'm rather busy right now," she apologized. She waved a graceful hand at the pile of papers beside her. "I have notes to write and a telegram to answer. You do understand, don't you?"

"Sure," said Kit, trying to hide her disappointment. She put away her pencil. "I'll come back another time."

A good reporter keeps on trying, Kit told herself, and she knocked on the door of the large dressing room labeled "Ladies." As the star of the play, Daphne had her own dressing room; this room was for all the other actresses.

"Come in," said a lively voice.

Kit entered and found Cecilia looking at herself in a full-length mirror. The young actress had light brown hair and a pink complexion, and when she smiled she had deep dimples in her cheeks. But she wasn't smiling now. She was frowning at her reflection. "None of the costumes fit me right," she complained, scowling down at the white satin gown she was wearing. "Daphne looks like an angel in this dress; I look like a dumpling."

Kit pulled out her pencil. "I was wondering if you could tell me what it's like to work in a professional theater."

Cecilia brightened immediately. "Oh, it's simply marvelous! Tons and tons of work, but a wonderful opportunity for my career! Of course, this isn't my first show. I acted in school, and I played professionally in a theater near Toronto for twelve weeks. But this is the first time I've had the opportunity to learn from experienced actors like Roland. And it's *such* an honor to work with Daphne. I'm her understudy, you know, and she's teaching me so much. I also play Lady Macduff, which isn't a very big part, but it's important because . . ."

Kit had to scribble as fast as she could to keep up with Cecilia's flow of information. She filled four pages in her notebook before Daphne Dumont's voice came from the private dressing room next door.

"Cecilia!" Daphne called. "Would you please come in here? I need help with these buttons."

"Must go!" Cecilia said brightly. She glanced at a clock on the dressing-room wall. "Oh gosh, it's past lunchtime!" Kit was startled to see that it was already two o'clock. She realized that Stirling had not yet arrived. He'd said he would come to the theater as soon as he finished his paper route, and she'd never known him to break his word.

Where is he? Kit wondered. She returned to the stage and Graham handed her another gallon of paint. "Where's your friend?" he asked her. "We could use his help drawing some of the castle scenery."

"I don't know," Kit answered. "He should have been here ages ago."

About half an hour later, Kit heard her name called in a low tone. She turned and saw Stirling standing in the shadow of the curtain at the edge of the stage. The theater was so filled with activity that no one else had noticed him.

Kit put down her brush and hurried over to him. Up close she could see that his knickerbockers were torn and dirty, his lip was bleeding, and there was a dark bruise around his left eye. "It was the Hobart brothers again, wasn't it?" she asked in a whisper.

Stirling nodded but didn't say anything.

"C'mon," said Kit. "I'll get you a glass of water."

She walked with Stirling down the stairs to the greenroom. At the back of the room, near the coffee percolator, several mismatched chairs were gathered around the old wooden table. Stirling sank gratefully into one of the chairs, careful to keep his back to the rest of the room.

Kit went to fill a mug with water from the ancient sink in the corner. As she returned with the water, Graham came striding into the greenroom. "You kids taking a break already?" he asked. His tone suggested that he didn't approve of breaks.

"We'll be out soon," Kit said.

Graham paused by the table. "You're not half bad as an artist, and we're short of help," he told Stirling, who was sitting hunched over. "Tell you what. I need ten more trees done by tomorrow. If you paint 'em all, I'll pay you fifty cents."

Kit, who had seen how long it took to paint a single tree, thought that the job was worth more than a nickel a tree. But Stirling brightened at the chance of earning money. "Sure," he said. He looked up at Graham and started to smile, but blood began to trickle from his lip.

Graham raised a single eyebrow when he saw Stirling's battered face.

"Um, I had an accident," Stirling mumbled,

hunching down in his chair again.

"I see," said Graham. The assistant manager grabbed a chair on the other side of the table and threw himself down on it. "You know," he said in a conversational tone, "fighting's not the best way to solve a problem."

Stirling took a gulp of water. Then he wiped his bleeding lip with the back of his sleeve. "How would you know?" he asked angrily.

Graham pulled out a clean handkerchief and handed it to Stirling. "I used to think I knew everything," Graham said with a smile. "About six years ago, I graduated from college and got a good job, and I was pretty happy with life." He leaned back in his chair. "Then the Depression hit. First I lost my job, then my apartment. Within two years, I was unemployed and sleeping in a shack in a Hooverville."

Graham paused, looking down at the scarred wooden table in front of him. "What happened next?" asked Kit, who was interested in spite of herself.

"One night, another hobo tried to steal my shoes. We got into a fight. A cop came by, and the other guy claimed that I'd attacked him. The judge believed the other guy, and I spent six weeks in jail."

Kit saw Graham finger the scar that ran up his cheek. *He looks like he's telling the truth,* she thought. *But there's no way to be sure.*

Graham continued, explaining that after he got out of jail, he was worse off than ever. He started riding the rails and wound up in Cincinnati, where the only work he could find was as an extra at the Burns Theater.

"Mr. Burns's health wasn't too good, and he needed an assistant manager. He ended up hiring me and teaching me everything I know about the theater." Graham stood up. "Mr. Burns also taught me to use my head, not my fists," he added, giving Stirling a playful punch on the arm. Stirling winced.

"Stirling doesn't *want* to fight," Kit protested. "Three brothers have been picking on him."

Mr. Bell came into the greenroom and overheard Kit's remark. The elderly man's face wrinkled with concern. "Are you all right?" he asked Stirling.

"Oh, he'll be fine," said Graham with a smile. He poured himself a cup of coffee and started heading back to the stage. "You've got work to do, right, Stirling?" he called over his shoulder.

"Right," said Stirling. He started to get up.

"Not so fast!" said Mr. Bell. He leaned down and examined Stirling's face. "You're going to have quite a bruise if you don't put some ice on that eye. And then what will your mother say when she gets home?"

Kit watched Stirling sink back into his seat with a worried look on his face. Stirling's mother had always believed that he was a delicate child who needed protection. Kit wondered what Mrs. Howard would do if she learned that Stirling was being picked on by bullies.

Mr. Bell dug into his pocket and pulled out a wallet. When he opened it, Kit saw with surprise that it was full of bills. *That's strange!* she thought with a start. *I didn't know that Mr. Bell had so much money.* Mr. Bell gave her a dollar and asked her to get a bar of soap to wash Stirling's cuts and a piece of ice to put on his bruised eye.

Kit headed out the back door of the theater and across the park. The sun was blazing down, but hopeful actors were still gathered in front of the theater. Kit was glad when she reached the shade of Maggiano's Grocery Store. She asked Mrs. Maggiano for the soap and the ice.

"You and Stirling been bothered by those Hobart boys again?" Mrs. Maggiano asked as she handed her a bar of soap.

"A little bit," Kit admitted.

Mrs. Maggiano shook her head sadly. "Ever since that family moved into the neighborhood, those boys have been causing trouble," she said.

"Do you know where they live?" asked Kit, thinking that she and Stirling should probably avoid that street.

"Yeah, they bought the Fitzgeralds' house, over on May Street," said Mrs. Maggiano. She chopped off a chunk of ice and then wrapped it in newspaper. "That'll be fifteen cents," she said.

Kit pulled out the dollar that Mr. Bell had given her. As she was about to hand the bill to Mrs. Maggiano, Kit noticed that part of it was tinted pink. She stopped. Her hands were damp with sweat as she examined the worn dollar more closely. A corner of the creased bill was missing and there was a definite pink tinge on one side.

"That'll be fifteen cents," Mrs. Maggiano repeated. Reluctantly, Kit handed her the dollar.

As Kit stepped back outside into the broiling sun, she felt cold fear inside, as if she had just swallowed the whole chunk of ice. She was almost sure that the dollar bill she'd given to Mrs. Maggiano was the same dollar she had used to pay for the theater tickets. But Mr. Bell had said that all the bills were stolen from the box office that night.

Why was the dollar in Mr. Bell's wallet? Kit worried. *And why does he have so much money?*

8

AN ACCIDENT?

At dinnertime, Kit and Stirling walked home from the theater together. They were both tired, but they walked fast, keeping their eyes out for the bullies. Only when they were finally in sight of Kit's house did they relax enough to talk.

Kit decided to share her concerns with Stirling. She told him all about finding the dollar bill. "And Mr. Bell didn't even get paid this week, but today his wallet was filled with money," she added. "Don't you think that's strange?"

Stirling frowned for a moment. "Mr. Bell would never steal anything," he said slowly. "I'm sure of it."

"I don't think he would either," Kit agreed.

"But how did that dollar bill get into his wallet? I'm almost sure it's the one I paid for our tickets with."

"Mr. Bell might not have had enough change in the cash box, so he put in his own money," Stirling suggested. "Then, later, he took some money from the cash box to pay himself back." He looked eagerly at Kit. "That could've happened."

Kit thought about it for a moment. "You're right," she said finally. "It must've been something like that. But *somebody* stole money from the box office. Maybe it was Graham, just like Sven said. Graham did spend time in jail."

"You heard him explain that," Stirling protested. "It wasn't his fault."

"We don't know that he's telling the truth," Kit pointed out.

"Well, I believe him," said Stirling. "He's going to pay me for painting those trees." Suddenly, Stirling looked guilty. He glanced over at Kit. "I'm sorry I haven't had time to draw pictures for your story yet. I still will if you want me to, but I've been busy with the trees."

"That's all right," said Kit, who'd been busy, too. "I'll bring my camera tomorrow and take pictures outside when the actors practice fighting with swords. That ought to make a good illustration."

"Yeah," agreed Stirling, brightening. "Graham said I could come out and watch the sword fighting, too." As they walked along, Stirling pretended to thrust and parry with an imaginary sword. Finally, he said, "I don't think Graham *could* be the thief. He's always thinking of ways we could make the play better. Why would he steal from the theater?"

Kit had an uneasy feeling in the pit of her stomach. "I don't know," she admitted. "But Graham *is* the only tall, thin man in the cast. Sven and Gunnar are both tall, but they're big. Roland Fairchild isn't thin, and he only looks tall onstage. He must wear special shoes or something, because in real life he's sort of short."

"Maybe the thief wasn't anyone from the cast," Stirling suggested, still continuing to fight with an imaginary sword. "The thief might've come from the outside and given Dionysius a bone so he wouldn't bark."

"Maybe," said Kit doubtfully. She and Stirling were almost home now, and Aunt Millie was picking tomatoes in the garden. Kit didn't want Aunt Millie to overhear her suspicions, so she didn't say anything more. But privately, Kit decided that she should watch Graham closely. *He's too good an actor,* she thought. *He seems to be telling the truth— even when he's lying.*

When Kit and Stirling walked in the back door, they were met by the spicy smell of tomatoes and herbs. Kit's mother was in the kitchen, cooking a pot of tomato sauce. Mrs. Kittredge looked questioningly at Stirling's blue-black eye and swollen lip.

"Is there anything you should tell me about, Stirling?" she inquired gently.

"No, ma'am," said Stirling. "I'm fine, really."

Then he escaped up to his room.

Mrs. Kittredge turned to Kit. "Well?" she asked, arching her eyebrows.

Why do I always have to explain everything? thought Kit, staring down at the linoleum floor. *It's not fair!*

A moment later, she looked up. Her mother was still standing there, waiting for an answer. "It's not really Stirling's fault at all . . ." Kit began.

Briefly, Kit explained how Stirling had gotten into a fight. "Mr. Bell washed the cuts and put an ice pack on Stirling's eye," she finished.

"I suppose that's all we can do for now," said Mrs. Kittredge with a sigh. "But Stirling's mother is *not* going to be happy when she sees his black eye." Mrs. Kittredge wiped her hands on her tomato-stained apron. "I'll talk to your father about it when he gets home. In the meantime, we'd better get dinner ready."

Kit stayed in the steaming kitchen to help her mother. She snapped the heads and tails off the green beans her mother was going to cook, and then she gathered up the silverware to set the table.

"I suppose Mr. Bell won't be home for dinner, will he?" Kit's mother asked.

"No, he's staying late to work at the theater," Kit told her as she counted out the knives, forks, and spoons. "There's a lot to do before *Macbeth* opens."

"Ah, well," said Mrs. Kittredge, stirring the pot of tomatoes. "At least he has enough money to buy himself dinner."

Kit remembered the bills she had seen in Mr. Bell's wallet. "He does?" Kit asked, trying to make her voice sound casual. She had overheard her mother and father talking about finances, and she knew that Mr. Bell had been behind on his rent. Her parents liked Mr. Bell, and they hadn't wanted to press the old gentleman, but the money he'd owed had been a strain for the family's budget.

"Yes, thankfully," Mrs. Kittredge said. She replaced the lid on the pot, and then added in a lower voice, "Yesterday, he gave us his past rent and paid the next two weeks in advance, too." She smiled at Kit. "I suppose everyone at the theater was finally paid."

Everyone except Mr. Bell, thought Kit as she finished setting the table. She remembered how Mr. Bell had refused to take his share of the week's profits. All through dinner she worried, *Where did he get the money?*

Stirling came downstairs for dinner, but he hardly said anything during the meal. As soon as it was over, he hurried back to his room again. After dinner, Kit's parents, Aunt Millie, Mrs. Dalrymple, Miss Jemison, and Mr. Peck all gathered on the front porch to enjoy the evening breeze. "Let's have some music!" Kit's father suggested.

Mr. Peck, who played the bass fiddle, announced that he'd just bought a violin, too. "I'm looking forward to trying it out," he said. "Would you like me to play a few tunes while you sing?"

The others agreed enthusiastically, but Kit

quietly slipped away, saying she was tired.

As she climbed the stairs to her attic bedroom, Kit heard the sweet, clear notes of the violin playing "My Wild Irish Rose." The song reminded her of Rose Burns, who was struggling so hard to keep the Burns Theater going—despite the stolen money.

Climbing into bed, Kit once again thought about Mr. Bell's wallet full of cash. She told herself that Mr. Bell couldn't be the thief.

She remembered how at mealtimes, Mr. Bell would never take second helpings of anything. Instead, he would offer his extra portions to Kit or Stirling. "You're growing children," he would urge. "Why don't you have it?"

Mr. Bell would go out of his way to help other people, too. He was always happy to pick up groceries for Kit's mother, and he often volunteered in the garden, helping Aunt Millie with the heavy digging, pruning, and weeding. He'd even helped Kit's father repair the old fan in Kit's room.

Mr. Bell never would've stolen a hundred and

fifty dollars! Kit thought as she felt the cooling breeze from the fan. But then she remembered Aunt Millie's words: "Desperate people sometimes do desperate things."

Someone was desperate enough to steal from the box office, Kit thought. *But who?* She decided she had to find out.

❖

In the morning, Kit fed Felix and watched him flit around the plants in his bowl. Looking at the little fish, Kit remembered that she'd gotten a letter from Ruthie, and she owed her friend a letter back. Kit took a fresh piece of paper and sat down at the kitchen table. She started her letter by saying that Felix was fine. Then she told Ruthie about the Hobart brothers and how they had been bullying Stirling.

Next, Kit chewed her pencil for a moment, wondering what she should say about the events at the theater. Should she tell Ruthie about the *Macbeth* jinx—or the theft at the box office? So much had been happening that Kit didn't know where to begin. *I guess it hasn't been as boring here at home as I thought it would be,* Kit realized.

Finally, she decided just to write, "Some scary things have been going on at the Burns Theater. I can hardly wait till you get home so that I can tell you all about them. Your friend, Kit."

Then she added: "P.S. I got Daphne Dumont's autograph for you. I'm taking my camera to the theater today, and I'll try to get a picture of her, too."

Kit mailed her letter on the way to the theater. She arrived early, and Graham immediately put her to work painting sets onstage. There were lots of new faces in the theater. Six actors and three actresses had been hired for the smaller parts in *Macbeth,* and they were busy learning their roles. A seamstress, Mrs. Panagoulas, was helping with the costumes, and the elderly woman had spread her materials all over the table in the greenroom.

Stirling arrived about an hour after Kit did. He was breathless, but he looked happy. "I sold all my papers this morning, and so did Vinnie," he told Kit in a low tone. "Just as we were finishing up, the Hobart brothers came after us, but we got away in time."

Around noon, Graham appeared onstage dressed in a long-sleeved white shirt and black pants. He was wearing a sword strapped to his side, and with his dark hair and the scar running down his cheek, he reminded Kit of a pirate in a movie.

Graham announced that it was time for the actors to go out and practice the play's sword-fighting scenes. "You come, too," he said to Stirling, handing him one-page announcements of *Macbeth* printed on thin paper. "I want you to pass these out to everyone who comes to the park."

Kit picked up her camera. "I'd like to get pictures for my article."

Graham thought for a moment. "Not a bad idea," he said grudgingly. "Come on."

Kit and Stirling followed the actors outside to a large grassy area in the park. Graham rolled up his sleeves and, with the help of Sven and Gunnar, began to teach the art of stage fighting. First, Graham gave a lecture on safety. Then he handed out weapons: wooden swords to the new actors; metal swords with covers on the ends for Sven, Gunnar, and himself.

"It's too bad they're not using real swords," said Stirling.

"At least they look real," said Kit. She watched Graham demonstrate different techniques, using Sven as his opponent. After each demonstration, the actors divided into pairs and practiced the moves until Graham called them back for more instruction.

It was the lunch hour, and many people were strolling through the park. Some of the passersby stopped to watch the actors. Aware of their audience, the actors began to fight more dramatically. The swordsmen yelled as they went on the attack and groaned when they pretended to be hit.

A crowd began to gather. Stirling walked around, handing out flyers to all the onlookers. As Kit stood on the edge of the practice area, she heard people talking about the play. "Isn't that the show that's supposed to be jinxed?" one woman asked.

"Nobody believes in jinxes nowadays," her male companion replied. "But I wouldn't mind seeing the fight scenes. These guys are pretty good."

Kit circled the practice area, looking for a picture that would show the men fighting but wouldn't be blurred by too much action. She snapped several photos, hoping that one or two would capture the excitement of the battles.

She was ready to click another photo when she saw Stirling through the lens. He looked scared and angry at the same time, and for an instant Kit couldn't understand why. Then she shifted the camera slightly and saw the white-blond hair of the Hobart brothers. The two younger boys stood on either side of Stirling, and they were holding his arms pinned behind his back. The oldest brother had the stack of flyers in his hands. He was grinning nastily and dangling the flyers just beyond Stirling's reach.

On impulse, Kit snapped a photo of the bullies. Then, her camera banging against her chest and her heart thumping loudly, she made her way over to them.

"Why don't you leave him alone?" Kit demanded of the oldest boy.

"Ooooh, Elton!" said the middle boy in mock fear. "I think she's trying to scare us!"

"Good thing for her that she's just a girl!" sneered the shortest boy.

Elton Hobart ignored his younger brothers and turned on Kit. "You better mind your own business," he told her. "'Cause if you don't—"

But before the boy could finish his threat,

a gasp went up from the crowd surrounding the swordsmen.

"Good heavens!" a woman cried. "That man's bleeding!"

"How awful!" exclaimed another woman.

In the confusion, Stirling pulled his arms free from the bullies. He and Kit rushed over to see what had happened. Kit heard Graham saying, "It's only a scratch—really. I'll be all right."

Graham was grasping his chest, and a red stain was spreading on his white shirt. Kit heard the other actors talking. They said that Graham and Sven had been demonstrating a tricky technique when Sven's sword had accidentally struck Graham under the ribs.

"I'm sorry!" Sven exclaimed in his booming voice. He looked worried. "I don't know how it happened." He put his arm around Graham's shoulders and helped him walk toward the theater. Kit and Stirling followed close behind.

"Shouldn't we call a doctor?" Kit asked.

"No, I'll be fine," Graham insisted. He told Gunnar to carry on with the lesson. "And you," he said, pointing to Stirling, "keep passing out the flyers."

Reluctantly, Kit returned with Stirling to the park. She and Stirling discovered that the Hobart brothers had scattered *Macbeth* flyers all over the grass, but the brothers themselves had vanished.

Kit helped Stirling pick up the flyers, and then together they distributed them through the crowd. As word of Graham's accident spread, more and more people stopped to watch the actors. "Maybe the show really is jinxed," said one young man who was watching the fighters from under the shade of a tree.

"I'd like to see it and find out for myself," his friend replied.

After they passed out their entire stack of flyers, Kit and Stirling headed back to the theater. "I hope Graham's all right," said Stirling as they climbed the metal stairs to the theater's back entrance.

"I bet he's back at work already," said Kit, trying to be cheerful. Yet as she walked into the greenroom, she sensed that something in the theater had changed.

9
THE CLUE IN THE ATTIC

Kit could hear actors onstage, rehearsing their lines, but the greenroom itself was strangely quiet. No fans were humming; no coffee was perking on the electric hot plate. The table had been cleared of Mrs. Panagoulas's sewing, and now assorted candles and lanterns were piled in the center of it.

A child with short, light brown hair was sitting at the table, hunched over a script. Before Kit or Stirling could say anything, the child stood up and pointed at them, announcing in a loud voice, "Thou *liest*, thou shaghaired villain!"

Kit was startled. "What'd you say?"

"I said, 'Thou *liest*, thou shag-haired villain,'" the child repeated, looking up at

Kit with large blue eyes. "Or do you think it should be: 'Thou liest, thou shag-haired *villain'?*" the child said again, this time putting the emphasis on *villain*. "I'm still memorizing the lines, and I haven't figured out exactly how I'm going to say them."

"Oh," said Kit, suddenly understanding. "You must be in the play."

"Yes," said the child, thrusting out a hand to Kit in a very grown-up way. "I'm Christina Tucker. I play Macduff's son, fourth act. It's a small role, not my usual sort of thing at all. I die after just a few lines, like this—"

Christina closed her eyes and clutched her chest dramatically. Then, groaning, she slid to the floor. A moment later, she popped up again. "Not bad, was it?" she asked. "Anyway," she continued, brushing off her white shirt, "Mother says it's good for my career to do Shakespeare, especially with Daphne Dumont."

Stirling looked baffled. "But how can you play Macduff's son?" he asked. "You're a girl."

"I play lots of boys' roles—that's why Mother keeps my hair short," Christina confided. "I can easily play a boy, as long as he's my age or a little younger. Watch me!" Christina scowled and made her hands into fists. She looked exactly like an angry young boy. Then she giggled and plopped back into her chair. "Of course, I like playing girls better. I get to wear beautiful wigs. I have one that makes me look just like Shirley Temple. Want to see me dance?"

Before Kit or Stirling could answer, Christina jumped out of her chair again and did a little tap dance on the greenroom floor. When she was finished, both Kit and Stirling applauded.

A voice came from the hallway. "That's enough, Christina—you don't want to tire yourself out. We have to leave right now to get to your next audition." A woman in a pink suit and bright red lipstick came in from the stage exit. Kit recognized her. She was the same woman who had been in line outside the theater and had told Kit that there weren't any parts for young girls.

"I'm ready, Mother," Christina said dutifully. She picked up her script just as Daphne and Graham were walking into the greenroom. "Good-bye, Miss Dumont!" Christina called as her mother hurried her out the door. "I'll see you tomorrow!"

Stirling turned to Graham. "Are you all right?" he asked anxiously.

"Yes, it was just a scratch," said Graham, waving away Stirling's concern. "I'm fine."

"How can anyone be fine under these conditions?" snapped Daphne. "You can't really expect us to put on a play in a theater without electricity. We have no lights, no fans, it's beastly hot in here, the seamstress can't see to sew, and I can't even see to put on my makeup. It's absurd!"

That's why it seems so different in here! Kit realized. *The electricity is off!*

"Don't worry, Daphne," Graham assured her. "The theater just got a little behind on paying the bills, so the electric company's shut off our power for a few days. But Rose is going to talk with them tomorrow. She'll convince them to turn the power back on."

Daphne shook her head sadly. "I really think this theater must be jinxed. One thing after another is going wrong." She looked up at Graham. "Why don't you just cancel the whole production? If you don't, something terrible could happen to all of us."

Kit felt a shiver go up her spine at Daphne's prediction. But then an even more terrible thought occurred to her. *What if they cancel the show? Then all the hard work would have been for nothing.*

Rose strode into the room. "We're not canceling anything," she said briskly. "And all this talk of a jinx is nonsense. The show must go on—and it will."

"You couldn't get audiences to come to *A Midsummer Night's Dream*," Daphne protested. "What makes you think they'll come to the Scottish play done in a dark theater?"

"We'll have the electricity back on by opening night," Rose promised.

"We'll have audiences, too," Graham added. "We've been getting some good publicity, and I had an idea: on opening night, we should offer fifty-cent tickets for everyone."

"Don't be ridiculous!" fumed Daphne. She whirled into her dressing room and slammed the door.

Rose frowned. "Why'd you have to make Daphne angry with such a silly suggestion?" she asked Graham. "Don't we have enough problems?"

"I was serious," said Graham. "We *should* sell all the tickets for fifty cents. We could pack the theater on opening night and make a nice profit."

"If we sell tickets for only fifty cents, we'll get people who've never even seen a Shakespeare play before," Rose objected. "They might start booing and hissing!"

"Don't be such a snob," Graham told her. "Rich people aren't the only ones who enjoy

Shakespeare. Your father always said that Shakespeare is for everyone."

"I'm *not* a snob!" Rose exclaimed. "But I *am* the manager of this theater."

"And it would be great publicity for the theater," countered Graham.

Kit thought of Aunt Millie and decided to speak up. "I bet there are a lot of people who love Shakespeare but can't afford to pay two dollars for a ticket," she said. "If there were fifty-cent tickets one night, maybe those people could come see the play, too."

"Exactly!" agreed Graham.

Rose looked from Kit to Graham. "I'll consider it," she promised.

"You'd better decide soon," Graham warned her. Then he clapped his hands. "All right, everybody. Let's get back to work!"

Kit returned to painting scenery, but whenever she had a chance, she interviewed members of the cast. First, she talked to Gunnar and Sven. She learned that they had been orphaned as children and had worked together ever since. Gunnar, the older of the two brothers, said that someday he wanted to retire from acting and buy a dairy farm.

Sven, on the other hand, dreamed of a career in the movies. "If I can ever make it to Hollywood, I'll be a star, you wait and see," he told Kit, speaking without a trace of his Swedish accent.

Later in the afternoon, Kit had a chance for a brief interview with Roland Fairchild. As he smoked a cigar in the greenroom, Roland told her how he'd performed in theaters all over the country. "I once played Hamlet in Washington, D.C.," he said proudly. "The President himself sent a note to me after the performance, saying it was the best he'd ever seen."

"President Roosevelt?" asked Kit, scribbling fast in her notebook.

Roland shook his head sadly. "No, it was before President Roosevelt's time." He looked down at Kit's notepad. "You needn't say which president it was, my dear. Just say 'the President.'" Roland stood up. "Well, I must be getting back to the rehearsal now," he said, stubbing out his cigar.

Kit went back to the scenery. As she swished bright gold paint across a throne made of wood, she heard the actors practice their lines. Some of the speeches were repeated so many times that Kit learned them by heart.

Throughout the rehearsal, Graham and Rose kept arguing about how the play should be presented. Graham wanted to have the ghost make its entrance by flying on lines above the stage. He suggested it might be nice if the three witches could fly in, too. "Your father always used to have dramatic touches like that," he advised Rose. "And the audiences loved 'em."

"This is a serious play, and I want to present it just as Shakespeare wrote it," Rose insisted.

"Serious doesn't have to mean dull," Graham argued. "Your father—"

Rose interrupted him. "I don't care how my father *used* to do things," she said firmly.

"I'm in charge now, and I have my own way of doing things."

As the afternoon light faded, the theater's few windows no longer illuminated the old building. Rose passed around candles and lanterns and warned everyone to be careful. "This is an old wooden building," she cautioned. "It could go up in flames very easily."

Kit continued to work onstage while the witches and soldiers practiced their lines by candlelight. Yet soon the light onstage grew so dim that she could no longer see what she was painting. Kit decided that she'd better work on reading *Macbeth* instead. So far, she and Aunt Millie had made good progress reading the play, but Kit still had more to go.

She asked Rose for a copy of the script, but Rose said all the copies were being used. "You can borrow my father's old copy. It has his notes in it and they may be helpful to you for your article," Rose offered. "It's a red leather volume and it's in the icebox in my office."

Kit decided to ask a question she had been

wondering about. "Why did he keep plays in an icebox?"

"Those plays were his most valued possessions," Rose said. "He kept them in the metal icebox so that if there was ever a fire in the theater, the plays might still survive."

Kit picked up a candle and went into Rose's office. Searching through the icebox, she found a lot of Shakespeare's plays, but not *Macbeth*. She went back to the stage and told Rose that the play was missing. Rose frowned. "Then Graham probably has it in his room," she said. "Look up in the attic. He lives up there to save on rent."

Gathering up her candle again, Kit headed through the greenroom. Stirling was at the far end of the room. He had set two lanterns on the table, and, kneeling on the floor, he was painting a tree. Kit opened the closet door, passed through the hanging clothes, and then opened the secret door that led up the stairs.

It was dark on the stairs, and for a moment Kit considered going back and asking Stirling to come with her. Then she felt silly. *There's nothing to be afraid of,* she reminded herself as she climbed the narrow, creaking stairs.

When Kit reached the top, she turned to the right. The attic's high, round windows faced east, and they let in only a glimmer of light from the setting sun. Kit held up her candle, and she could see the neatly made bed and the desk with a chair. Everything looked as it had two days ago, except that a white shirt was hanging over the back of the chair.

Kit saw a book bound in red leather on top of the desk. She picked it up and looked inside. *"Macbeth"* was printed in large letters on the title page, but the page was also filled with handwritten notes. Kit was about to close the book when one of the notes caught her eye. Holding the candle close, she read the script carefully. It said: *Macbeth = Accidents.*

Even though the attic was hot, Kit felt a chill. She looked more closely at the shirt that was hung over the chair. There was a large red stain on it. With a shock, Kit realized that it must be the shirt Graham had been wearing when he'd had the sword-fighting accident.

Kit started to turn away, but then she noticed that something about the shirt looked wrong. Shadows danced on the rafters overhead as she brought her candle up to get a better look. The stain was bright red. *Don't bloodstains turn brown as they dry?* she wondered.

There was a funny smell in the air, too. Kit bent down closer, careful not to touch the shirt, and sniffed. It smelled like ketchup.

Graham lied to us! Kit realized with a shock. *He wasn't hurt at all—he just used ketchup to make it look like he'd been wounded!*

Warm wax from the candle dripped on Kit's hand as she stood up, but she hardly even noticed it. Her mind was whirling. Why had Graham faked his accident? Could he really be trusted at all?

Just then Kit heard the door at the bottom of the stairs creak open. She caught her breath.

She couldn't let Graham discover that she knew his secret.

In an instant, she blew out her candle and dove behind a musty-smelling trunk. Crouched in the dark shadows, she heard footsteps on the attic stairs.

10

SMOKE

Kit held her breath and listened hard as the footsteps grew closer. Then, to her great relief, a familiar voice called out, "Kit, are you up here?"

It was Stirling. Kit saw the light from his lantern, and she allowed herself to breathe again. "I'm over here," she said, coming out from behind the trunk. She was surprised to hear that her voice sounded normal.

Stirling turned his lantern in her direction. "What are you doing up here?"

"Um, I was looking for something," Kit said. *That's mostly true,* she thought.

"Well, I saw you come up, and I wanted you to know that Graham said everyone should break for dinner. We'd better go home."

Kit could hear Graham's voice downstairs. He was telling the actors to be back in an hour. "Don't be late," he warned them. "We have a lot of work to do."

Kit tucked the copy of *Macbeth* under her arm. "Let's go," she told Stirling.

When they got downstairs, Kit saw that the newly hired cast members had all gone home. Only the core actors were still in the theater. They had gathered in the greenroom and were discussing what to do for dinner. "I wish we could eat here," said Gunnar, casting his eyes yearningly toward the electric hot plate in the corner. "Sven and I are trying to save money and—"

"We'd all like to save money," Roland interrupted. "But with the electricity off, we can't cook here. So I vote we go to the Greek diner. They're having a special."

Most of the cast members decided to go with Roland, but Graham shook his head. "I'm not hungry," he said. "I'm going to stay here and work."

The thought of Graham alone in the theater made Kit uneasy. *I wonder if he's going to try some other trick,* she thought. Kit felt better when Daphne said that she was going to stay in the theater, too. "I'll be in my dressing room, going over my lines," she told the others. She handed Mr. Bell some money. "Would you pick me up my usual fruit plate on your way back?"

In his courtly, old-fashioned way, Mr. Bell said that he would be more than happy to be of service. Then he turned to Kit. "Please give my best regards to your parents and tell them I shall return late tonight."

"Yes, sir," said Kit. She felt her stomach twist with worry as she looked up into his kindly blue eyes. *If Mr. Bell is a thief,* she thought, *I don't think I'll ever be able to trust anyone again.*

As she was leaving the theater, Kit decided to put the copy of *Macbeth* where it would be safe. She carefully tucked away the leather-bound volume in a corner of the ladies' dressing room, and then she and Stirling went home for dinner.

But by the time they reached home, dinner was over. Kit's parents, Aunt Millie, and the boarders were gathered on the porch to enjoy the cool evening air. Kit's great-uncle, Hendrick, was visiting, too. He sat on the most comfortable chair, with a plate of sugar cookies and a glass of lemonade beside him. He frowned at Kit. "You completely missed dinner tonight, didn't you, young lady?"

Kit explained that there was a lot to be done at the theater and most of the cast members, including Mr. Bell, were planning to work very late. "May Stirling and I stay late tomorrow night?" she asked her father. "We're helping with the sets."

Kit's parents exchanged a glance. Then Mr. Kittredge nodded. "All right," he said. "But walk home with Mr. Bell. I don't want you and Stirling walking home by yourselves late at night."

"Humpf!" grunted Uncle Hendrick. "I don't

know why you children are wasting all your time with this foolishness at the theater," he complained. He brushed cookie crumbs from his vest. "You should be doing something useful."

"But the theater *is* useful, Hendrick," Aunt Millie declared as she darned the worn-out heel of one of Kit's socks. "A good play is like food for the soul. We all need it."

"Our *stomachs* need food, not our souls," Uncle Hendrick declared. He reached for another cookie.

"Well, President Roosevelt thinks differently," said Aunt Millie. "That's why he's starting up the Federal Theatre Project. It's going to help support unemployed actors and bring plays to people all around the country."

"I've never heard of anything so stupid in all my life!" Uncle Hendrick exploded. "Every decent American ought to write to the newspapers and protest. The government has no right to spend taxpayers' hard-earned money for a lot of foolish entertainment!"

"Speaking of entertainment, why don't we have some music?" Kit's mother broke in cheerfully. She turned to Mr. Peck. "Would you play your violin for us again?"

Mr. Peck agreed. He left the porch and a few minutes later returned holding a violin made of lustrous chestnut-colored wood. Mr. Peck ran his bow across the violin's strings, and it gave off sweet, pure music.

"That's quite an instrument you have there," said Uncle Hendrick. He sounded as if he was impressed despite himself.

"Thank you, sir," said Mr. Peck with a nod. "I've never owned anything so fine in all my life. It belonged to Mr. Bell's late wife, Elena. He had long known that I admired it, and this week he agreed to sell it to me."

Kit's heart gave a jump. "You bought the violin from Mr. Bell this week?" she asked.

"Yes, on Monday, as a matter of fact. It took every penny I had in savings, even though Mr. Bell was kind enough to offer it to me at a very reasonable price. He said he wanted Elena's

124

violin to go to someone who'd appreciate it." Mr. Peck looked lovingly at the beautiful instrument. "And I truly do."

As the singing began on the porch, Kit and Stirling headed toward the kitchen for their dinner. "That must've been where Mr. Bell got his money!" Kit whispered as they made their way down the hall.

"Yeah, and that proves he's not the thief," agreed Stirling. "If he'd stolen the money from the box office, he wouldn't have had to sell his violin."

Kit nodded, smiling. She was so relieved to know that Mr. Bell was innocent, she practically skipped into the kitchen. She and Stirling found plates of meat loaf, corn, biscuits, and sliced tomatoes waiting for them on the kitchen table. There was also a letter addressed to Stirling, and he opened it eagerly.

"It's from my mom," Stirling said after a few minutes. "She's coming home on Friday." He looked across the table at Kit. "Do you think she'll notice my black eye?"

Kit studied his face. Stirling's eye had turned a dark shade of purple. "Well," she said, hoping for the best, "Friday is still two days away. Maybe it'll be better by then."

Stirling folded up his letter and returned it to the envelope. "We've got a whole lot to do at the theater before Friday," he said, pouring some ketchup on his meat loaf. "The trees are taking me a lot longer than Graham thought they would. I hope he's not going to be mad."

Kit lowered her voice. "I don't think we can trust Graham," she said. She told Stirling about the suspicious stain she had found on Graham's shirt. "He wasn't hurt at all—it was just an act. And it was a mean trick to play on everyone."

For several moments, Stirling stared down at his plate. He pushed his corn around with his fork, not saying anything. Finally, he looked up at Kit. "Maybe Graham had a good reason," he said. "We don't know for sure."

"No," Kit agreed. "But we know that someone stole money from the theater, and

Graham's our best suspect. We know he doesn't always tell the truth. And today he faked an accident. Maybe he doesn't want *Macbeth* to be a success."

"All right," Stirling said slowly. "We'll keep an eye on him."

The next morning, while Stirling was selling his newspapers, Kit sat in the living room with Aunt Millie. Together, they finished reading the last act of *Macbeth.* "Oh my gosh!" Kit said as she finally closed the book. "I liked it, but it was *so* sad! And so many people died."

"Well, it *is* a tragedy," said Aunt Millie. This morning she was darning the elbow of a sweater, and she sewed tiny, neat stitches as she talked. "The tragedies show us mistakes people make in their lives—and maybe teach us to not make those same mistakes ourselves."

"But Macbeth was ready to kill people just so he could be king," Kit pointed out. "Not many other people would make a mistake like that!"

"No," Aunt Millie agreed. "But maybe you've known someone who put his own ambition above everything else? Who didn't care what he had to do as long as he achieved his goals?"

Kit thought immediately of Graham—how he had lied to the debt collectors, how he had faked the sword-fighting accident, and how he was always forcing everyone in the cast to work harder and for less money than they thought possible.

"I don't know," she told Aunt Millie slowly. "Maybe."

Kit thanked her aunt for her help. "I think I'll be able to write my article now. It's due at noon tomorrow, so I'd better start work on it. I need to help get things ready at the theater, too. Tomorrow is opening night!"

"Waste not, want not," Aunt Millie reminded her with a smile. "So you'd better not waste any time."

SMOKE

Kit gathered up all her notes and the spool of film from her camera. She left her film at Murphy's Drugstore to have it developed. Then she headed to the theater. As she approached the back of the building, she saw that a truck had pulled up to the basement entrance. A heavyset man wearing a tan cap was standing by the truck talking with Graham. Neither man seemed to notice Kit as she climbed the outside stairs.

Kit overheard the man warning Graham, "This stuff is dangerous. You can get burned pretty bad, so you got to be careful how you handle it. Be real careful how you store it, too."

"Don't worry—I know what I'm doing," Graham told him.

When she reached the top of the stairs, Kit stopped and looked down. She saw Graham and the heavy man unloading two boxes from the truck. But the men still hadn't seen her. Kit slipped into the theater, and then opened the door just enough so that she could look outside.

A Thief in the Theater

She felt a chill of fear as she watched Graham and the other man disappear into the basement. *What's Graham doing?* she wondered.

But Kit didn't have time to wonder for long. As soon as she went onstage, Rose asked her to help finish painting an outdoor scene. "Use this for the sky," Rose said, pointing to a bucket of dark blue-gray paint. "It should look as if it's going to storm any minute."

Since the electricity was still off, the theater was hot and only dimly lit by the windows. As Kit worked onstage, she noticed that everyone was on edge. Roland snapped at Daphne. Daphne seemed distracted and was always forgetting her lines. Sven shouted at the swordsmen when they tripped over each other during the battle scene. Even Cecilia was grumpy, and she burst into tears for no apparent reason.

When Graham finally called a break around noon, Kit was glad to put down her paintbrush and pick up her reporter's notebook. She waited until Daphne finished her scene with

Roland, and then she asked, "May I interview you now, Miss Dumont?"

Daphne smiled regretfully. "I'm afraid not, dear. Maybe another day."

Kit looked down at the pencil she was holding in her paint-spattered hand. This was the third time she'd asked Daphne for an interview, and each time the answer had been no. Kit gathered her courage and tried again. "I don't want to bother you, but I won't be able to do it another day, because I have to hand in my article tomorrow, so—"

"I'm sorry, darling, but I have a terrible headache," Daphne interrupted. She was frowning. "It's this awful heat. I really must go lie down. I can't possibly talk with you today."

I guess I won't have an interview with the star after all, Kit thought as Daphne walked off-stage.

"Why don't you interview me?" a voice asked. Kit turned and saw Christina Tucker sitting at the edge of the stage, with a script open in her lap. "I'd like to be in the newspaper. Would you put my picture in, too?"

Kit laughed. "I don't know about a picture, but sure, I'll interview you." Kit opened her notebook to a fresh page of paper and sat down beside Christina. "First, tell me how to spell your name and how old you are."

"C-h-r-i-s-t-i-n-a T-u-c-k-e-r," she spelled. "Only when I play a boy, I'm known as 'Chris Tucker,' and I'm eight."

"How many plays have you been in?"

"Fourteen!" Christina declared.

Kit poised her pencil above the paper. "Fourteen?"

"I've been working in the theater since I was two," Christina said proudly. She leaned over confidentially. "Mother says that I could be the next Shirley Temple."

Kit was writing as fast as she could. "What's it like to work in a professional theater?"

"It's a job," said Christina with a frown. Suddenly she looked much older than her eight years. "Sometimes it's fun. But sometimes, I wish I could just play outside instead and—"

Before Christina could continue, Mrs. Tucker called from the other side of the stage. "Christina, dear! We have to be at your next audition in half an hour! And then we have to get back here again for the rehearsal. So let's hurry!"

As Christina rushed offstage, Kit decided she'd use her free time at lunch to get one more interview. The door to Rose's office was ajar, and Kit knocked on the glass panel.

"Yes?" said Rose. She looked up from her papers and Kit could see that there were dark circles under her eyes. "What can I do for you, Kit?"

Kit explained that she was finishing her research for the article and wanted to ask a few more questions. Rose glanced at her watch and said she had a couple of minutes before she needed to prepare for the dress rehearsal. Kit quickly pulled out her notebook.

"How long have you worked in the theater?" Kit asked.

"I've been in theater all my life," said Rose. She kneaded her forehead with one hand, and she looked more tired than ever. "When I was a baby, I used to sleep in a cradle backstage while my mother was onstage acting. I've lost count of how many plays I've been in, but it's a lot."

Kit jotted down her answer and then asked, "How did you decide to become a theater manager?"

Rose thought for a moment. "Well," she said, "one year I thought everyone had forgotten my birthday. But when I got home, my mother said, 'Surprise!' She and all her friends had decorated our apartment, and they put on a musical show just for me."

Suddenly, Rose smiled so widely that her whole face lit up. "It was magical! For one afternoon, I felt like the most important person in the whole world. I think that's when I decided that *I* wanted to put on shows for people, too."

Before Kit could ask any more questions, Rose stood up and said it was time to get ready for the dress rehearsal. "And we'll need your help in the greenroom," she told Kit.

It took a long time to get everything ready. Kit helped by sewing on stray buttons and finding props for the actors. Stirling kept busy painting the final touches on the scenery. When the rehearsal finally began, it went painfully slowly, with Rose sometimes repeating a scene several times.

By the time the actors were halfway through the play, Kit had finished all her chores in the greenroom. Since no one needed her help, Kit decided it was time to work on her column. She retrieved the copy of *Macbeth* from the ladies' dressing room, and then, borrowing a lantern from the greenroom, she slipped into the theater and looked around for a quiet place to write.

Kit saw rows of empty seats in the darkened balcony. Venturing up the thickly carpeted stairs, she found a seat in one of the small, curtained boxes that overlooked the stage. The velvet-covered seat was soft and comfortable, and Kit had a wonderful view of the stage. She could look out over the balcony railing and see the actors performing, but unless the actors looked very hard, they couldn't see her.

Working by the light of the lantern, Kit started to write the first line of her article. "A play..." she began.

Then she stopped, not sure what to write next. She tried several different opening sentences, and she wasn't happy with any of them. Finally, she put down her pencil and watched the rehearsal, hoping it would give her an idea for the article.

As Kit watched the action onstage, however, she became increasingly worried. The actors kept standing in the wrong places and saying the wrong lines. To make matters worse, only lanterns and candles lighted the theater, so everything seemed dark and depressing.

Kit knew that her editor, Mr. Gibson, wanted cheerful stories for the children's page. But she also knew that the first and most important job of any reporter was to tell the truth. *What can I write about?* she wondered.

She tried writing several paragraphs and crossed them all out. She was still rewriting the first paragraph when the rehearsal ended. It had taken almost four hours to rehearse the two-hour play, and it was now well past dinnertime. From her balcony seat, Kit watched the cast gather onstage, and she decided to go downstairs and join them.

As she approached the stage, Kit heard Graham announce that the cast could take a break. "You"—he nodded at Christina, who looked half asleep—"can go home, but I want everyone else back here after dinner. We have a lot more to do tonight."

"What about the lighting?" Roland asked. With a sweeping gesture, he pointed to the dark theater. "We have no spotlights, nothing to work with!"

"I'm going to talk to the power company again in the morning," Rose promised. "I'm sure I can get them to listen to reason."

"What if you can't get them to change their minds?" Daphne demanded.

Rose lifted her chin defiantly. "People were putting on Shakespeare's plays long before there was electricity. If they could do it, so can we."

There was a murmur of concern among the cast, but it soon gave way to a discussion of dinner. Most of the actors decided to go to a German restaurant that was having a "Wurst for Less" night. Both Rose and Graham, however, said they would be staying in the theater. Rose had paperwork to do in her office, and Graham said he had set planning to finish. With a tired smile, Daphne said that she would be resting in her dressing room.

"Would you like me to bring you your usual dinner?" Mr. Bell asked her.

"No, not tonight, thank you," said Daphne. "I'm not hungry. I have a splitting headache."

SMOKE

Kit joined Stirling in the greenroom as the actors were filing out to dinner. "My dad said we could stay late," she reminded him, and she took out the cheese, lettuce, and tomato sandwiches Aunt Millie had packed for them.

Kit and Stirling ate their sandwiches at the table in the greenroom. After dinner, Kit realized that she'd left her notebook and the copy of *Macbeth* up in the balcony box, and she had to go get them. "I haven't been up there yet," said Stirling, picking up a candle. "I'll go with you."

The empty theater was oddly quiet as they made their way up the stairs by the flickering light of Stirling's candle. When they reached the box, Stirling was impressed by the view. "You can see everything from up here," he said. "Look, there's Graham."

Kit turned around and peered out over the balcony railing. She saw Graham carrying a brown box onto the stage. It looked like one of the boxes that had been delivered that morning.

"That's strange!" she murmured.

"What?" Stirling demanded.

In a low voice, Kit explained how she had seen the boxes delivered. "The truck driver said that the stuff inside the boxes causes burns and can be really dangerous."

"I wonder what it is," said Stirling.

"I wish I knew," said Kit. She watched Graham put down the box and then leave. A few moments later, he brought one of the giant witches' cauldrons onto the stage. Then he disappeared again. When he returned, he was carrying a pail and a pair of tongs. He put the tongs down on the floor of the stage. Lifting up the pail, he poured a liquid from it into the cauldron. Then he stepped back for a moment.

Kit felt a rising sense of dread. She saw Graham look around the theater, as if to be sure that no one was around. Both she and Stirling pulled further back from the railing, and Kit shaded the candle with her hand. "I don't want him to see us," Kit whispered to Stirling.

SMOKE

"What do you think he's doing?" asked Stirling.

But Kit didn't answer. Her eyes were fixed on the stage. She watched Graham pick up the pair of tongs. Using the tongs, he reached into the box, pulled something out, and tossed it into the cauldron.

Kit's fear turned to terror as a fog of smoke erupted on the stage.

11
A CONFESSION

Kit felt sure that the entire theater was going to go up in flames. She and Stirling ran down from the balcony. "Fire!" Kit yelled as they raced down the stairs toward the main floor.

"Help!" Stirling hollered.

Graham emerged from behind the smoke. Jumping down from the stage, he ran toward Kit and Stirling. "What's happened?" he shouted.

Rose rushed in from her office. "Where's the fire?" she yelled. Dionysius followed close behind her, barking excitedly.

"There!" Kit pointed to the billowing smoke on the stage. Then, to her amazement, both Graham and Rose began to laugh. Dionysius stopped barking and settled himself down on the theater floor.

"What?" said Kit.

"What's so funny?" Stirling demanded.

"That's not a fire," said Graham, still laughing. "It's a special effect that I'm going to use to make the cauldrons look spooky onstage."

Kit felt her face grow hot with embarrassment. "It *looked* like something was on fire," she insisted.

Graham explained that the effect was caused by solid carbon dioxide—usually known as dry ice. He was using it to produce a fog of mist designed to look like smoke.

"I was just checking to make sure it was convincing," he said. He chuckled again. "I guess it was."

"Oh!" said Kit, suddenly feeling very foolish. She told Graham how she had overheard the truck driver's warnings about danger and burns.

"Dry ice *is* dangerous," Rose interjected. "It has to be stored and handled very carefully.

And it's so cold that it can 'burn' you if you touch it." She turned to Graham. "You *were* being careful, weren't you?"

"Of course I was," Graham said. He paused and looked from Kit to Stirling. "But why were you two up there watching me, anyway? I thought you'd gone home."

"I'd left my notebook in the balcony. When I went to get it, we saw you onstage and we thought—" Kit stopped. Then she swallowed hard, unsure what to say next. She glanced over at Stirling, and he was staring down, as if hoping that the theater floor would open up and swallow him.

"Well, what'd you think?" Graham asked impatiently.

"We, uh, thought you might be playing a trick again," Kit admitted.

Rose lifted her eyebrows. "What kind of trick?" she asked.

A look of alarm passed over Graham's face, and then he smiled. "Aw, they're just kidding." He gave Stirling a hearty slap on the back. "Come on, let's get back to work."

"Not yet," said Rose. She turned to Kit. "What did you mean when you said he might be playing a trick again?"

Under Rose's penetrating gaze, Kit explained how she had gone to Graham's room to borrow the copy of *Macbeth.* "I saw the stain on the shirt that you were wearing when you had the sword-fighting accident," she told Graham. "Only the stain was ketchup, not blood, so I knew the accident was a trick."

"Oh, for heaven's sake!" Rose exploded. She turned on Graham. "You said you just got a tiny scratch. But that whole thing was an act, wasn't it?"

Graham glanced around the empty theater. "Look," he said to Rose. "Why don't we all go into your office? We can talk in more privacy there."

"Fine!" said Rose. She led the way to the crowded little office off the lobby, with Graham, Kit, Stirling, and Dionysius following close behind. After Rose shut the glass door,

Graham confessed, "Okay, I faked the accident. Sven and I practiced it ahead of time till we got it just right."

He grinned at Rose. "Your father was the one who showed me the old ketchup trick. It worked like a charm."

Rose sighed. "I should have guessed," she said. "And I suppose you were responsible for that 'accident' after *A Midsummer Night's Dream,* too? It was awfully convenient for the scenery to collapse just after I announced *Macbeth.*"

"Sure, I planned that too," said Graham. "As soon as you told me that you wanted to do *Macbeth,* I arranged for the arch to fall down and for Cecilia to fake a twisted ankle. I even thought ahead and got a doctor friend of mine to be in the audience. It all went pretty well, I thought," he added proudly.

Stirling looked up at him anxiously. "You didn't steal the money from the box office, though, did you?" he asked.

"Of course not!" said Graham. "And

nobody was hurt by any of the accidents—
I made sure of that."

"But why?" asked Kit. "Why pretend
that the *Macbeth* jinx was causing so much
trouble?"

Rose shook her head. "Because he's following my father's tradition," she explained. "My
father used to always stage little 'accidents'
with *Macbeth* in order to get more publicity for
the play."

"Your father knew about theater," declared
Graham. "And the accidents did just what they
were intended to do." He reached over and
picked up the *Cincinnati Daily Herald* story
and waved it in Rose's face. "Half the city has
heard about our production now, and they'll be
lining up to see it!"

Rose grabbed the newspaper and tossed it
down on the desk. "I told you that I wanted
to produce the show my own way—without
any cheap tricks," she said. She stared up at
him, her hands on her hips and her eyes flash-
ing with anger. "And if I could play your role

in *Macbeth* myself, I'd fire you right now!"

Kit had a hard time imagining Rose, who was small and slender, playing the role of a Scottish warrior. But then she remembered Christina, who would be playing a young boy.

Suddenly an idea occurred to her. "Oh, no!" she gasped.

12

MIGHTIER THAN THE SWORD

Rose and Graham both turned to Kit. "What?" they demanded.

"Well," Kit said slowly, "men used to play all the women's parts in Shakespeare—and women now sometimes play men's parts, right?"

"I know," said Rose with a sigh. "But I wasn't serious about taking Graham's role."

"That's not what I meant," said Kit. She felt the idea bubbling up inside her. She continued, talking quickly now. "Remember how Mr. Bell said he saw a tall, thin young man leaving the theater the night that the money was stolen?"

Stirling understood immediately. "You think that maybe it wasn't a man at all—

maybe it was a woman dressed up to look like a man?"

"It's possible," said Kit excitedly. "Maybe we should've been looking for a tall, thin *woman*."

"Even if it's true, I don't see how that helps us," said Rose. "Cecilia's not tall *or* thin. In fact, the only woman who fits that description is—"

She paused for a moment, and she and Graham looked at each other. Then together they said, "Daphne."

"She's certainly the only one around here with any cash," Graham said thoughtfully. "While the rest of us are all living on the cheap, she's staying at a fancy hotel. She's always giving old Bell money to go buy her meals, and today she had him send a telegram for her, too."

"That's right!" Kit exclaimed. She remembered how the dollar she had paid at the box office had turned up in Mr. Bell's pocket. *Maybe Daphne's the one who gave it to him,* she thought. She caught Stirling's eye, and he nodded.

"We don't have any proof," said Rose. "But maybe we should go talk to Daphne. She was acting strange at rehearsal today, as if she didn't really care about the play anymore."

Graham and Rose headed to Daphne's dressing room, followed closely by Kit and Stirling, with Dionysius trailing along, too. Rose knocked sharply on the door. There was no answer.

"Daphne!" Graham called out in his most authoritative tone. "Are you in there?" There was still no answer.

Rose tried the door, but it was locked. "Let me get my keys," she said.

"Don't bother," Graham told her. "These locks are ancient." He pulled out a long, slender file, twisted it in the lock, and then opened the door. The first thing Kit noticed was that the window leading onto the fire escape was wide open and the curtains were fluttering in the breeze. *Oh no!* Kit thought. *We're too late!*

Kit looked around the room. It still smelled of Daphne's perfume, but the star's clothes and makeup were gone. The wastebasket was overflowing with trash, and it looked as if Daphne had cleaned off the dressing table in a hurry. All that was left on the table was a tired-looking bouquet of flowers and a note written on Daphne's monogrammed notepaper.

Graham picked up the note and read it aloud:

To whom it may concern,

I regret to inform you that the conditions at this theater—including no electricity, reduced pay, and lack of a professional manager—make it impossible for me to carry out the terms of my contract.

"Well, of all the nerve!" interrupted Rose. "What does she mean by 'lack of a professional manager'?"

"Listen to the rest of it," said Graham. He read:

I have therefore decided to end my association with the Burns Theater and pursue other, more rewarding theatrical opportunities elsewhere.

Farewell and good luck,
Daphne Dumont

"Well, now our Lady Macbeth is gone," said Graham, folding up the note. "And tomorrow is opening night."

Kit looked at the lines of concern on the faces of Rose and Graham. "You're not"—she hesitated—"going to cancel the play, are you?"

"Of course not!" exclaimed Rose, looking fierce. "*Macbeth* will go on tomorrow night even if I have to stand on a dark stage and play every role myself!"

"That won't be necessary," said Graham drily. "Cecilia can play Lady Macbeth—she knows the role and she'll be thrilled to have her first big break. Since she's from Canada, we can even advertise her as an 'internationally known actress.'"

"All right then, that's settled." Rose nodded.

"Now I'm going to go find Daphne at her hotel. I want to talk with her about the missing money." Rose turned around and started heading toward the greenroom.

"Wait!" said Graham. He pointed to the open window. "Looks to me like Daphne left by the fire escape. If so, she went to a lot of trouble to avoid us. I don't think she'll be sitting at her hotel, waiting for us to come visit. She's probably already packed her bags and is on her way out of town."

"Taking our money with her," Rose said bitterly.

For a few moments, there was a heavy silence in the room. Stirling was the first to speak up. He'd been looking at the overflowing wastebasket. Now he pulled out a crumpled sheet of paper. "Here's a train schedule. Maybe she's gone to the railroad station."

"The trains run all night," Graham said thoughtfully.

"It's worth a try," Rose agreed. "Let's go."

Kit jotted a quick note to Mr. Bell, telling

him that she and Stirling would be back soon. Then she met Rose, Graham, and Stirling on the sidewalk outside the theater.

"Do you have enough money for a cab?" Rose asked Graham as her high heels clicked on the cement.

Graham shook his head. "No."

"Neither do I," said Rose. "So I guess we'll walk."

They hurried through the steamy evening to the Union Terminal. Kit could see the bright lights of the station from several blocks away. Inside the beautiful domed building, Kit felt overwhelmed by all the people. Red-capped porters were toting trunks, businessmen were rushing to catch trains, and families were standing in line, holding tight to old suitcases and boxes tied with twine.

"Where do we start?" asked Stirling as they stood in the middle of the station. "She could be anywhere."

Graham suggested that they split up. He and Rose took the left side of the station, while

Stirling and Kit took the right. "Look every-
where," Rose instructed them. "We'll meet
back here in the middle."

Kit and Stirling slowly walked through the
station, past the shoe-shine men and the cigar
sellers, and past all the people lined up in front
of the ticket booths. They carefully checked the
benches filled with travelers waiting for trains.

They had reached the far end of the station
when Kit saw a slim woman sitting in the corner with two suitcases by her feet. The woman
was turned away from the crowds and she had
a hat pulled low over her face, but there was
something familiar about her graceful posture.

"I think that's her!" said Kit, grabbing
Stirling's elbow. Together, she and Stirling
watched the woman for several moments. She
shifted position, and Kit caught a glimpse of
her face. It was Daphne.

"I'll get Graham and Rose," said Stirling.
"You make sure she doesn't go anywhere."

Kit continued to watch Daphne as Stirling
ran off. Suddenly, Daphne looked up and her

eyes met Kit's. A look of alarm flitted across the actress's face. She stood up and started picking up her suitcases.

Kit knew she had to do something. She hurried over and stood in front of Daphne.

"Hello," said Kit, desperately trying to stall for time. "Is your headache better?"

"Ah, yes it is, thank you," said Daphne, smiling. "What a surprise to see you here! But I must be going."

She really is a good actress, Kit thought. *She looks as if she's happy to see me.* Out of the corner of her eye, Kit saw Rose and Graham running over with Stirling. Kit waved to them. "Don't go yet," she told Daphne. "Rose wants to talk to you."

"I see," said Daphne, glancing over her shoulder. She sat down again. "Very well, I suppose I can spare a few minutes."

In a moment, the others arrived and stood breathless in front of Daphne.

Daphne smiled up at them. "I understand that you all want me to return to your little play," she said sweetly. "But you must see that your production is hopeless. Also, I received a telegram today offering me a wonderful theatrical opportunity in New York. So my mind is quite made up, and I'm afraid—"

"Forget it, Daphne," Graham interrupted. His voice was hard. "We know you stole the money."

She looked at him as if he had lost his mind. "I beg your pardon, but you know nothing of the sort! That's complete and utter nonsense!"

Daphne sounded sincere. *What if we're wrong, and she's not the thief?* Kit worried.

But Graham's face was stony. "We found a witness who saw you running out the front door that night. He recognized your face from a picture we showed him."

"But the hat—" Daphne began. Then she turned away. "I don't know what you're talking about," she concluded.

"We're talking about the money," said Rose. She held out her hand. "I want it back."

Daphne stood up. "You'll have to excuse me," she said with great dignity. "You have no right to speak to me so rudely, and I must go now. I have a train to catch to New York. As I told you, there is a very exciting theatrical opportunity waiting for me there."

Rose leaned toward Daphne and spoke very slowly and clearly. "If you don't give back every dollar you stole, I'm going to write to all the theater owners in New York and tell them that you're a thief. Then you'll see what kind of theatrical opportunities you get!"

Daphne looked at the four faces staring at her. She hesitated for a moment, and then she sat back down on the bench. "I didn't *want* to take the money," she said as she reached down and picked up her purse. "And I was planning to pay it back to you anyway."

Graham raised his eyebrows but said nothing.

Kit breathed a sigh of relief as she watched Daphne take a wad of bills out of her purse. "I have expenses," Daphne continued, as she

slapped the bills into Rose's waiting hand.
"And I knew from the start that your production of the Scottish play would be a disaster.
This money was just my insurance so that I
could get back to my agent in New York."

Slowly, Daphne counted out one hundred
and thirty dollars. "I'm keeping the last twenty
because you owe me that," she told Rose. "It
should have been my share from *A Midsummer
Night's Dream*."

"All right," said Rose, pocketing the money.
"But you know, the person you've really
cheated is yourself."

Daphne looked suspicious. "What do you
mean?"

"You missed out on the chance to star as
Lady Macbeth at the Burns Theater," said Rose,
holding her head high. "And you're wrong
about the production being a disaster—it's
going to be a hit!"

As they walked out of the station, Kit asked Graham, "Was there really a witness who saw Daphne steal the money?"

Graham winked. "No, but she didn't know that, did she?"

"Gee," said Stirling. "You seemed so sure—I believed you."

"Yes," Rose agreed. "For a moment, I almost believed you myself—you're not a bad actor." She hesitated and then added, "I'm sorry for what I said earlier about firing you."

"I never thought you meant it," Graham said confidently. "And you didn't do such a bad job yourself. Threatening to write to all the theaters was a brilliant trick." He grinned at Rose. "You know, your father always said that the pen is mightier than the sword. Maybe you're more like him than you realize."

"Maybe," Rose admitted with half a smile. She turned to Kit and Stirling. "Without you two, Daphne would have gotten away with it— and the money would've been on its way to New York by now." She looked at Kit. "I think you have a knack for investigating—you really could be a great reporter someday!"

Kit felt a glow of pride. Then she realized that tomorrow was Friday—and her newspaper article had to be on Mr. Gibson's desk by noon. Her stomach twisted. *What am I going to write?*

13

OPENING NIGHT

At eight o'clock the next morning, Kit was waiting at the door of Murphy's Drugstore. As soon as Mr. Murphy opened the store, she picked up her developed photos. Then she hurried outside to look at them in the sunlight.

She'd hoped that the photos would give her ideas for her article, but the results were a disappointment. None of the pictures she had taken inside had come out at all; the theater had been too dark. The pictures she had taken at the park were a little better, but they were much too blurred to be used in a newspaper.

With a sigh, Kit decided to go ask Stirling if he'd still be willing to draw a picture for the article. She found Stirling on his old street corner. He was carrying his bag of papers and yelling, "Newspaper! Get all the news Cincinnati wants to know!"

"None of my photos came out, so I need a picture before noon," Kit told him urgently. "Could you do a sketch of the stage? Or the sword fighting? Or anything you think would be good, really?"

Stirling nodded. "I'll get started on it as soon as I sell my papers," he said. "I promised Graham I'd help with the lights today, too. Now that Rose can pay the bill, they should have the electricity on by this afternoon." Stirling grinned. "And guess what—Graham is going to pay me today, so I'll have ten dollars to give my mother when she gets home!"

Kit thanked him and then turned to leave. But she'd gone only a few steps when she caught a glimpse of three familiar figures on the opposite side of the street. She whirled back to Stirling. "The Hobart kids are coming!" she warned him. "Quick! Let's get out of here!"

Stirling looked down at his newspaper bag.

It was still full of papers. "I can't," he said. "If I don't sell these this morning, I'll have to pay for them myself. And then I won't have my ten dollars anymore."

"Come on!" Kit urged him. "You can sell the papers somewhere else."

Stirling squared his thin shoulders stubbornly. "I was talking with Vinnie, and we decided we're tired of them pushing us around. We're not going to run away anymore."

"Well, if you're staying, I'm staying, too," Kit decided. Holding tight to her photos and the ten cents in change that she had gotten from Mr. Murphy, Kit planted her feet squarely on the sidewalk.

A moment later, the Hobart brothers arrived on the street corner. They circled around Stirling, taunting him. "Hey, kid!" the biggest boy said. "You know you gotta pay if you want to sell papers on our corner."

"Yeah," the youngest brother chimed in. "Give us a dollar or we'll give you another black eye." All three of the brothers laughed.

Stirling's face went pale, but his voice was deep and loud. "No! And you'd better leave me and Vinnie alone or we're going to the cops."

The oldest boy grabbed Stirling's shirt and picked him up. "It would be your word against ours," he warned Stirling. "And if you tell on us, you'll be sorry."

Kit felt anger churning inside her. She couldn't stand to see Stirling dangling help-lessly. It reminded her of the afternoon at the park when the Hobart boys had stolen Stirling's flyers. Suddenly, Kit remembered the photos she was holding.

"You'll be the one who's sorry, Elton Hobart," she told the oldest brother, saying his name in a loud, clear voice. "Because we've got these pictures!" She pulled out the developed photos and waved them in the air, being careful not to let the bullies see how blurry they were.

The boy dropped Stirling and turned his attention to Kit. "Pictures? What do I care about pictures?" he demanded.

"You should care," Kit told him, stepping backward. "Because I took these pictures of you at the park when you were picking on Stirling. They're all the proof that the police will need!"

"Let me see those!" said the boy. He lunged for the photos.

"No," said Kit, stepping nimbly out of the way. She thought up a quick fib. "And don't bother trying to steal them, either, 'cause I've got the negatives at home. I'll give a copy to the police, and if you ever bother us again, I'll give a copy to your mother, too! I know that you live on May Street, and I'll go right up and ring your doorbell."

The brothers looked at each other nervously. Kit wasn't sure what worried them more: the police finding out about their activities, or their mother learning about them. But whichever it was, the brothers started to back away from her.

"So you'd better get out of here now!" said Stirling with his fists clenched.

Elton shook his head in disgust. "Aw, I'm

tired of bothering with a pip-squeak like you anyway," he told Stirling. He gestured to his brothers. "Come on, let's go where there's some real money."

As the brothers walked away, Stirling shouted after them, "Next time you need money, why don't you work for it like everybody else?"

When the bullies were out of sight, both Stirling and Kit jumped up and down cheering. "It worked!" Stirling exclaimed. "I've got to go tell Vinnie!"

"And I've got to go home and write my story," said Kit. "I finally know what I want to write about." She hurried home and ran up the two flights of stairs to her room. Then she sat down at her desk and put a fresh sheet of paper in her typewriter.

```
    Putting on a play looks like
fun, but there's a lot of work
that has to be done before the
curtains go up . . .
```

Opening Night

On opening night, the Burns Theater was transformed. Lights shone brightly on the marquee, and a crowd of people lined up to buy the fifty-cent tickets. To thank Kit and Stirling for their work, Rose had given them six free tickets, and they had invited Stirling's mother, Kit's parents, and Aunt Millie as their guests. Uncle Hendrick had thought that fifty-cent tickets sounded like a good deal, and he'd decided to buy one and come along, too.

Kit and Stirling were waiting anxiously by the box office with their tickets in hand when their family members arrived. "Stirling, dear! How I've missed you!" Mrs. Howard exclaimed, running up to her son and giving him a big hug in front of everyone.

"Why, you've grown so much!" she declared, standing back and looking at Stirling carefully. "Oh dear! What's that bruise under your eye?"

Kit's parents exchanged a nervous glance, but Stirling just shrugged casually. "It's nothing, Mother, just a scratch," he said.

Mrs. Howard leaned forward to examine his eye more closely. "It looks like a nasty bruise." The lines of worry in her forehead deepened. "It's that newspaper job, isn't it? I worried about you so much while I was away. I was afraid something terrible would happen to you. You must quit that job immediately."

Stirling stood up straight. "Don't worry, Mother," he told her. "There was a problem, but my friends and I took care of it. And I'm making good money at my job. I saved up ten dollars for you while you were away."

Mrs. Howard blinked. "Ten dollars?"

"Yes, ma'am," Stirling said proudly. Then he offered his mother his arm. "Let's go into the theater."

The rest of the group filed into the theater, too, and Mr. Bell led them to the front-row seats he had been saving for them. As she looked around the theater, Kit was thrilled to see that all the seats were filling up—even those in the balcony.

But the best moment of all came when the curtain finally opened. The stage revealed an eerily beautiful forest with three witches bending over smoking cauldrons. The scene looked perfect, and a gasp of delight went up from the audience. Even Uncle Hendrick muttered, "Not bad!"

Mrs. Howard's eyes opened wide. "Oh!" she whispered. "It's magical!"

Kit looked at the witch in the middle of the stage. It was Rose, her face transformed by heavy makeup. Rose caught Kit's eye and gave her a tiny, almost imperceptible wink.

Then the play began, and Kit found herself being drawn into Shakespeare's world.

A play is like magic, she thought happily as she watched the witches through the mist of cauldron smoke. *The best kind of magic!*

Looking Back

A Peek into the Past

During the hard years of the Depression,
Americans were eager for the chance to forget
their troubles for an hour or two and be enter-
tained. There was no television in Kit's day,
but all through the Depression, children and
grown-ups alike gathered around radio sets and
filled theaters in record numbers.

Most people in the 1930s had very little
money, however, so entertainers often went to
great lengths to attract audiences, just as the
actors in Kit's story do.

Movie theaters drew millions of people
each week by cutting ticket prices
and offering great promotions.

For ten cents, a kid could watch a Saturday matinee, including *two* full-length movies (a "double feature"),

A theater advertises its special promotions.

a cartoon, a newsreel, and the latest episode of an adventure serial such

Movie audiences in Kit's time loved Tarzan, the ape-man.

as *Tarzan of the Apes.* Kids often got free ice cream treats, too.

In the evenings, movie theaters attracted grown-up audiences by offering wildly popular promotions—such as Bingo Nights with cash prizes, or Crockery Nights, when pieces of china were given away. Even more popular were Bank Nights, when the audience drew tickets to win cash prizes. By the end of the Depression, more than 100 million people had taken part in Bank Night promotions!

Radio was even more popular than movies, because it was free. There were all kinds of programs, from variety shows, westerns, and baseball games to radio versions of Hollywood movies and Shakespeare

Boys caught up in a radio show

plays. Many children loved adventure and detective series. Fans of the Orphan Annie adventure series could even order a special decoder badge to help Annie solve mysteries!

Radio and movies were so popular, in fact, that live theater had a hard time competing for audiences. Small theater companies, like the fictional Burns Theater in Kit's story, simply couldn't afford to sell tickets as cheaply as the movie theaters.

Fans of the Orphan Annie radio show sent in for this special Orphan Annie Decoder Badge!

So many live theaters went out of business that in 1935 the government created the Federal Theatre Project, or FTP. It was one

of the programs designed to help the millions of Americans who were unemployed during the Depression.

An FTP play in a New York park

The FTP gave jobs to unemployed actors, directors, playwrights, and stagehands across the country. It also created some of the most memorable theater of the 1930s, including a famous production of *Macbeth* directed by Orson Welles and performed by an African American cast.

Macbeth is the story of a Scottish general who is so ambitious for the crown that he murders the king as well as the innocent family of a rival.

*A scene and poster from the FTP's famous 1936 production of **Macbeth***

One of the changes that Orson Welles made in the play was that he set it on the Caribbean island of Haiti—a radical idea for the 1930s. The play was a huge success.

In order to stay in business during the Depression, theater companies *had* to be creative about promoting their plays. The actors in Kit's story certainly do that—by playing off people's fascination with spooky superstitions.

For some reason, superstitions are very common in the theater. Mr. Bell tells Kit one of the best known: Never wish an actor good luck before he goes onstage. Instead, say the opposite—"Break a leg!" Other common superstitions: It's bad luck to whistle in a theater, to say the last line of a play during rehearsals, or to have real food or money onstage. Many theaters, especially in

*A cat in a dressing room brings **good** luck!*

England, are believed to be haunted, and most theaters keep a "ghost light" always burning to ward off bad spirits.

The superstitions about *Macbeth* that Kit's friends at the Burns Theater use in their publicity stunts haven't disappeared, either. Even today, many actors and directors won't say the play's name inside a theater. They simply call *Macbeth* "the Scottish play" or even just "the play." Yet despite the superstitions, *Macbeth* is one of Shakespeare's most popular plays.

William Shakespeare lived from 1564 to 1616 and is widely considered the greatest writer in the English language. Today, just as in Kit's time, audiences around the world enjoy his plays.

A modern audience spellbound by **Macbeth**

ABOUT THE AUTHOR

 Sarah Masters Buckey grew up in New Jersey, where her favorite hobbies were swimming in the summer, sledding in the winter, and reading all year round.

Today, she and her family live in New Hampshire. She is the author of *The Light in the Cellar: A Molly Mystery* and two mysteries featuring Samantha Parkington: *The Curse of Ravenscourt*, which was nominated for the 2005 Agatha Award for Best Children's/Young Adult Mystery, and *The Stolen Sapphire*, which was nominated for the 2007 Edgar Award for Best Juvenile Mystery.

She also wrote three American Girl History Mysteries: *The Smuggler's Treasure*, *Enemy in the Fort*, and *Gangsters at the Grand Atlantic*, a 2003 Agatha Award nominee.